Flying for Frankie

Pauline Fisk is the much-loved author of eight children's novels, including *The Mrs Marridge Project*, *Sabrina Fludde* and *Midnight Blue* which won the Smarties Prize and was shortlisted for the Whitbread Children's Book of the Year Award. Pauline has five children and lives in Shropshire.

For Penny, who flew as well.

First published in 2009
by Faber and Faber Limited
Bloomsbury House, 74–77 Great Russell Street,
London WC1B 3DA

Typeset by Faber and Faber Limited
Printed in England by CPIBookmarque, Croydon

A CIP record for this book
is available from the British Library

ISBN 978–0–571–23619–0

2 4 6 8 10 9 7 5 3 1

Flying for Frankie

PAULINE FISK

faber and faber

Book One

The House on Clarence Street

My name's Charis Watts, which is sounded with a *k*, not a *ch* the way that Bryony Rogers does it to wind me up. My home's in Dartmouth, which my brother Damo reckons is a great place to retire to but the death of all hope if you happen to be under twenty-five. But I disagree. Dartmouth's what Damo made of it. If he chose to work the boats when he left school instead of becoming the blues guitarist he'd always wanted to be, no one was to blame but him. In fact, I said that once and I swear, if I hadn't been his baby sister, he'd have taken me outside.

Nowadays we live on Above Town in the house we bought from Henry Askew, who's one of the bosses where Dad works. But in the old days we lived on Clarence Street with Grandma, behind the whitewashed wall at the top of the hill. There's a blue door in that wall, opening inwards from the pavement, and we'd go through it and up a flight of stone steps and our front door would be straight ahead of us, up a metal fire-escape.

Grandma occupied the sunny side of the house, which I suppose was only fair, seeing as she was the one, not us, who'd inherited it from the Johncox family as thanks for all those years of service as a nanny. She had the rooms with all the best river views, and the only bit that we could see was from the attic, where I had my bedroom. The window was tiny, and too high to look out of from my bed. If I stood on a chair, though, I could see all the way past the fine old houses on the Dartmouth water-front to St Petrox's Church and the castle, where the river flows out into the sea.

I was born in Dartmouth, which means that ours is a proper local family with Dartmouth in our blood. We're not like some people, who have houses down here but live in London most of the time. Everybody knows us, which can be a bit claus-trophobic sometimes, but at least things aren't as bad as they used to be when Damo was still living at home.

Damo Big-Mouth – that's what I always called him, because he could never keep things to himself. It used to drive me crazy walking past the Dolphin, where Damo always drank, and the boys on the bench outside wouLd call, *Hey there, Damo's sister*, as if I didn't have a name of my own. I'd only have to be wearing a new pair of shoes and they'd know how much they cost, where they came from and the trouble I'd had persuading my skinflint dad to buy them for me.

Dad would probably kill me if he knew I'd bought myself a book and was writing all this down, and so would Damo. But there's a story inside me that I've got to tell, even if it means being a big mouth too. I've known I should tell it for ages and finally it's got to the point where, if I don't do something now, I'll forget half of the things that matter and they'll all be lost.

What I really want to write about isn't Damo at all, or Bryony Rogers, for that matter, so I don't know why I mentioned them. It's Frankie that I want to write about, and something tells me that it's going to take more than one small exercise book, bought at Pillar's the newsagents. Francesca Diana Bradley, to give Frankie her full name. She came barging into my life without warning or invitation, and ended up becoming my best friend.

The Bradleys live across the river from us. Theirs is the big house on top of Kingswear Hill (Bradley Castle, people call it) that looks one way out to sea and the other across the water to Dartmouth. People joke that with their tennis court, stable block, terraces and sweeping lawns, the Bradleys certainly know how to put the *king* into Kingswear. They say that, as you come into harbour, even at night time, Bradley Castle is the first thing you see. Nowadays the word is that the Bradleys are negotiating with the National Trust to buy part of the cliff top for a helicopter pad. But that's Dartmouth for you – always full of crazy stories. I don't believe it for one minute.

When we were small, Frankie's and my paths never crossed. I knew who she was, of course. I'd seen her enough times, driving off the ferry in one of her family's cars, or going up and down the river in one of their boats. People would say things like, 'There she goes, Little Miss Up-Herself.' But they didn't know what they were talking about. Underneath all that princess stuff, Frankie was a really down-to-earth, funny girl, and a loyal friend.

I know that now, but I didn't then. In those days, it wasn't just the rest of Dartmouth who called Frankie Little Miss Up-Herself. I did too.

Pink Flamingos

Frankie was born within days of me, but whereas I put in my first appearance in the cottage hospital on the Dartmouth waterfront (which was as far as Mum could get before I came hurtling out into the world), Frankie emerged into the private wing of the Royal South Hams.

In this, and every other way as well, there was no comparison between us. Frankie was the perfect baby who never cried, but I could have represented Britain in the baby-howling championships. She wore designer baby clothes. I wore other people's hand-me-downs. She was slim and golden, even as a baby apparently. I was curly and squat, and I stayed that way. (When Frankie insisted she'd give anything for my curly, dark looks, I knew she was lying to make me feel better.)

As we grew, the differences between us grew as well. Frankie's life was full of ballet, riding, water sports and tennis, whereas mine was full of loafing around doing nothing in particular. While Frankie was always being whisked off somewhere in her mother's car, as remote and mysterious as a princess, I'd be sitting in front of the telly, or trailing around with Damo until he shook me off.

My life was dull, but Frankie's was gilded. Her parents held champagne parties on their boat for everyone to see and hear on both sides of the river, and they were always going abroad on flashy holidays. Frankie's father was as tanned as a film star, her mother as sleek and elegant as a supermodel. Every weekend her brothers came home from boarding school for the family to go sailing together, or wind-surfing, or riding their horses.

You'd see them trailing around Dartmouth in their jodhpurs or sailing gear, swaggering from shop to shop as if they owned them all. The older brother was known as 'Gorgeous George'. The Dartmouth girls were all over him, and they were all over his brother, Diggory, too, though he was younger and reckoned not to be half as good-looking.

The first time I ever crossed paths with the Bradleys was in the organic clothing shop, Green Flax, where Mum used to work until she got her present job as a medical secretary at the Royal South Hams. On Saturdays and in the holidays, I'd hang around offering to help, but mostly getting under Mum's feet.

On the day in question, Gorgeous George came in, his little sister in tow, with a pair of loafers that he wanted changing. When he couldn't find his size, he demanded money-back. But Green Flax don't do money-back. They have notices about it all over the shop, but George got mad when Mum pointed them out and, when Mum wouldn't back down, Frankie got mad too. She obviously wasn't used to anybody saying no to the Bradley family. She even went so far as to swear at Mum – and then I got mad too.

'Hey, Little Miss Up-Herself – that's *my mother* you're talking to!'

I don't know why I did that. It's not like me to throw my weight around. Mum turned and glared, as if to say that she could handle this herself, thank you very much. But the damage was already done. Frankie looked stunned, as if she'd never been spoken to like that. Then George gave me a 'who the hell are you?' look, grabbed his sister's hand and went storming out of the shop, leaving the loafers behind. He swore they'd never come back, and neither would anybody else from their family, or their friends and neighbours or anybody else they knew.

'Do you realise what you've done?' Mum said, after they'd gone. 'That family spends a fortune in this shop. You never, *ever*, talk to a customer like that!'

After that – as if it was my doom – I couldn't get away from Frankie. She wasn't just 'the Bradley girl' any more. She was a person I'd crossed swords with – and she turned up everywhere I went. I'd only have to be strolling past the Dart Marina Hotel, and she and her mother would be sitting on the terrace having coffee. Or I'd linger outside the hairdresser's, wishing I could afford to go in and get my curls straightened, and Frankie would be there having her blonde hair highlighted.

Why she bothered, I didn't know. She had hair to die for – long, thick, straight and naturally blonde. But she was never happy with it. Even though I didn't know her, that much was plain to see. She was always fiddling with it, and she had this way of pulling it over her face and then flicking it back – something I never understood until I saw her with school friends one day, and they were all doing it.

Frankie went to a school that was full of girls like her, with flicked-back hair. I guess it was some tribal habit. You could pick out the girls from that school simply by the flick. When you saw them all together with their long legs, pink skin, long necks and flicking heads, they looked like a flock of flamingos.

In fact, that's what I called them. *The flamingos.*

There was nothing to choose between them. I never thought of them as people who might be like me. Have the same feelings. Share any of the same hopes and dreams. And I certainly never thought I'd make friends with one of them. Not in a million years.

But that's exactly what I did. And this is how it happened.

Castle Cove

Castle Cove's the sort of place where anything could happen, even something as unlikely as Francesca Diana Bradley and me becoming friends. It's my favourite bit of Dartmouth – always has been, always will be – and it's where I am now, writing all this down.

For years, people passing on the cliff path never even knew that Castle Cove was there. It used to be my private place, which no one could get down to except me. People know about it now, because the steps have been repaired, the DANGER sign has been removed and a post has been erected, pointing the way down. But for years I had it to myself.

I even made a den down there, built among the roots of an old tree that grew out of the cliff. The tide had this way of washing things in just when I needed them. Once, when I got the idea of making a platform up in the branches of the tree, it brought me a wooden pallet and a coil of rope. Then another time, when I was worrying about camouflage, it washed in a massive piece of netting that I draped over the den and covered with grass, seaweed and bracken.

In fact, I was working on my camouflage the first time Frankie went past. A shame I didn't do it sooner, that's what I thought. Frankie was out with her brothers in their father's boat, churning up the water in the bay and sending seagulls squawking up the cliff. When I heard them coming, I stood as still as a rock face, hoping they wouldn't notice me. But they must have noticed something because, a couple of days later, Frankie returned.

She was on her own this time, and in a little sailing dingy that I never noticed until too late. I looked up from making a wind chime out of bits of flotsam and there she was, pulling the boat up the beach. She'd already seen me and I knew there was nothing I could do. My day was ruined. I wished I hadn't come. There was nowhere I could run to, nowhere to hide, nothing I could do but watch Frankie walk towards me, the expression on her face telling me that she knew I was the girl who'd called her Little Miss Up-Herself.

'Hey, you – what do you think you're doing?' she cried as she approached. You'd have thought Castle

Cove was some private Bradley beach and I was trespassing.

I didn't answer, but then I didn't really need to. Already Frankie had swept past me. Telling her to get off my property had no effect. The Bradleys weren't the sort of people who needed permission to go anywhere, and Frankie was no different to the rest of them.

As if she owned it, she started poking around in my den. I followed angrily.

'What d'you think *you're* doing?' I said.

But Frankie didn't answer. She was too busy sticking her nose into everything. There was nothing I could do to stop her. She climbed up onto the platform and I hoped it would collapse. Then she climbed down again and dug around in the roots, finding the place where I hung my posters of Johnny Depp dressed as Captain Jack Sparrow.

'You don't fancy him, do you?' she said.

I could have died. 'What's it to you?' I said, turning bright red.

Finally I managed to get Frankie out of the den, even though I couldn't get her off the beach. She stood staring back at the den, and I could have sworn I saw envy on her face.

'Did you do all that yourself?' she said.

'What if I did?' I replied.

'Well, if you did, I've got to say you're brilliant,' Frankie said. 'Never in a million years could I have created something like that. It's easily the best den I've ever seen. Although it could do with a bit of furniture. And some rugs might make it cosier. And, when it comes to posters, you could most definitely do better for yourself than Johnny Depp.'

I flushed again. As if she hadn't noticed, Frankie started on about furniture her family was putting out that I could have if I wanted. No one would mind, she said. It wouldn't even be missed. I only had to say the word and she could ferry it round.

I told her I wasn't interested but next day, despite what I'd said, the furniture started arriving. I tried to make Frankie take it back, insisting I didn't need it, but she lined it up on the beach and went off for more. Either she was mounting a takeover, I decided, or trying to wind me up for calling her Little Miss Up-Herself.

When the next lot arrived, I said again that the den was fine without furniture and, besides, it was mine, which meant it wasn't her place to decide what went in it. But Frankie refused to take anything back, saying that, if I didn't want it, I could let the tide carry it away.

Soon the beach was full of furniture. There was nothing I could do to stop it coming. It was good stuff too. After Frankie had finally departed, I tried out a couple of wicker armchairs, marvelling at anybody wanting to put them out. Then I examined a table with a carved top. Then, finally, I unrolled a couple of threadbare Persian-type rugs and unpacked a stack of long velvet curtains. But I wouldn't put any of them in the den.

I didn't see Frankie for a couple of weeks after that. Eventually she returned but, by then, the table had been washed away and so had the curtains. Not that she made any comment. Instead, she came ashore, waving as if we were old friends.

I remember watching her, my heart sinking. I'd hoped I'd seen the last of her, but it seemed not.

'Hi,' she called.

'What do you want?' I replied, as suspicious as ever. But, by the end of that day, we had become friends.

How it happened I'm still not quite sure. To begin with, I tried ignoring Frankie. Then I tried being rude to her. Then I even tried to set her boat adrift, though without success. She sat at one end of the beach and I sat at the other, and slowly it came to me that a den with nobody in it but me wasn't half as much fun as one that could be shared.

By the time Frankie left that night, we'd hauled the furniture inside and started the process of transforming the den into a home-from-home. But, more than that, we'd started to transform ourselves. Because somehow, beyond what either of us had expected, we'd discovered something in each other – a shared loneliness, maybe – that had brought us both to life.

Later, Frankie said that making friends had never come into it – she'd only bothered to get to know me because she wanted my den. But I knew that she was winding me up. Something genuine sprang up between us that day in Castle Cove, and it wasn't just a five-minute wonder either. It was something we both stuck with. Something that, over time, simply grew and grew.

Right from the start, though, our friendship had to be a secret. From that first day onwards, both of us understood that telling our families was not an option. The Bradleys would never approve of their princess of a daughter keeping company with some local girl whose parents were always out at work, leaving her to hang about Dartmouth from dawn to dusk. And I knew that if Damo ever found out, he'd embarrass me all over town, mouthing off about my closeness to Little Miss Up-Herself.

I remember Frankie and I talking about it one day – marvelling at the way, after all this time, we'd still managed to keep our friendship secret. We were walking round St Petrox's Churchyard, reading inscriptions on graves, and Frankie said that, once you died, all your secrets died with you.

'I think it's sad,' she said. 'Once you go, so does everything you've ever done. The world carries on as if you'd never even existed. All that's left is a stone – and stones keep their secrets to themselves.'

I said that, when I died, I didn't want a stone at all, but to have my ashes scattered across Castle Cove. Frankie said she'd like that too but, knowing her luck, she'd end up in some massive family vault with railings round it and a statue of herself lying like a Tudor princess.

It was the only time I'd ever heard her joke about her family's aspirations and the crazy way they threw money about. I joked as well, saying that, if anyone in our family died, they probably wouldn't get even a headstone because Dad was too stingy to blow his money on the dead.

'If he dies first, Mum's going to spend his precious savings all in one go,' I said. 'That's her big secret. She says she's going to *spend, spend, spend.*'

The Day We Talked About Blood

Things started changing the day we talked about blood. It was the weekend of the Dartmouth Music Festival. There were bands in all the pubs and concerts in the bandstand. The streets were heaving with buskers and every available open space had a musical event taking place. There were people milling everywhere, plastic beer glasses in their hands. Music was coming out of doors and windows all over town.

Even St Petrox's Church, down next to the castle, was swinging to the beat of some visiting London gospel choir. I could hear them from the den, where I'd gone to get away from Damo, who was swaggering all over town, trying to get in on other people's acts.

I hadn't expected Frankie to be there but the first thing I saw, as I climbed down the broken steps, was her boat, and I hadn't got much further before she came running to greet me. Her parents were out and her brothers, who were meant to be looking after her, had gone to the music festival instead. So we had the afternoon to ourselves.

We spent the whole time in a world of our own. And I mean that quite literally – in a real world of our own. Over time, Castle Cove had transformed from private beach to make-believe kingdom to secret world. Once it had been just a beach with a tree at the top of it with the right-sized roots and branches to turn into a den. But, over time, it had become a country with boundaries, border posts and entry rituals that could never be divulged. The den was now a castle with lookout posts. It even had a throne room, where we, its queens, were crowned, and the whole place was governed by a parliament that we took turns to be in charge of as prime minister.

We never gave our kingdom a name, but we did give it a secret language. 'Laftish' was the word we used to describe the beauty of a day when the sun shines and everything goes right. 'Hangly' meant sad. 'Clugs' were people who spoil your fun. 'Clugging' meant being dragged away reluctantly, against one's will. And the word 'mesmiritious' brought with it a sense of contentment so great that it simply couldn't be improved upon, 'I'm feeling mesmiritious' being as good as anything could ever get.

And that's how it was that afternoon, hanging posters of men, including Frankie's favourite, Orlando Bloom, in the throne room and sunbathing on a slab of rock. I remember the cliff above us being a mass of wild flowers and new green leaves. I felt wrapped up in a living, breathing world of sunlight and sea.

It was only when the sun started lowering that either of us realised how late it was. We didn't want to leave but knew we had no choice. Even I, whose parents rarely seemed to question where I was, knew that some explaining would have to be done.

Usually Frankie and I would go our separate ways right there on the beach, me climbing the broken steps and walking home, and Frankie crossing the water in her boat. Because it was so late, though, she transported me upriver to the higher ferry at the top end of Dartmouth, which was as near as she could get me to Clarence Street.

I remember us being out on the water, the evening sun shining down the river, making it look like a piece of crumpled cellophane. Frankie was quiet all the way, which wasn't like her, because she was usually such a talker. Her expression was set in marble and I wondered if something other than being late was bothering her.

We approached the higher ferry and she still hadn't said a word, so I asked if everything was all right. She said it was, but perhaps she said it too quickly or something, because the words rang hollow. Then, when we got up to the landing jetty, she said something else, and suddenly it was one of those conversations that you never forget.

I could hear blues music coming from the Dart Marina Hotel, which lies just beyond the ferry terminal. Now, every time I hear its sad, straining notes, Frankie's words come to mind.

' I think I might have started my periods,' she said. I don't know for sure, but nothing else makes sense.'

I remember my first reaction was, 'Is that all?' But my second reaction was envy. Suddenly it looked like Frankie was a grown-up, proper woman and I was left behind.

'What makes you think you've started?' I said, trying to disguise my true feelings.

'I don't know,' Frankie said. 'I could be wrong. But I'm getting spots of blood every time I pee, and if it's not my periods I don't know what else it might be.'

We'd reached the quay by now. Frankie leapt out, tied up the boat and held it steady for me to climb out too.

'If you're bleeding, you must have started your periods,' I said. 'Do you have any pain?'

I hoped she did. When she pulled a face, I remember feeling glad. Was pain conclusive evidence, she asked – as if *I* knew anything.

'Why are you asking me?' I said. 'I'm hopeless at that sort of thing.'

When I've got time, I'll give you all the details of my sex education, courtesy of Mum. It won't take long, believe me.

Frankie got back into the boat. She was beginning to look as if she wished she hadn't mentioned the subject. I felt ashamed for being sharp with her.

'You're growing up,' I said, in what I hoped was a softer voice.

'It doesn't feel like growing up to me,' Frankie replied.

'What does it feel like, then?' I asked.

Frankie looked strangely blank. 'I don't know,' she said, as if genuinely perplexed. 'That's the trouble. It feels like nothing. It's hard to explain. A great big nothing inside of me, which should feel exciting and yet it doesn't. In fact, I don't know why I mentioned it. It's probably nothing. Forget I ever said anything.'

Alf Resco's

The next time I saw Frankie was in the dark cavern at the back of Alf Resco's Coffee House, which was where we'd meet sometimes after school, tucked right at the back next to the coffee machine. We ordered milkshakes with cream and chocolate shakes on top and sucked them slowly through ice-clogged straws. It was ages since we'd seen each other, and to begin with Frankie was her usual self, full of funny stories about girls in her class. Finally, however, she ran out of things to say and I asked about the periods.

Frankie blushed, hushing me with a glance. They were fine, she whispered, but could I not shout from the rooftops? She didn't want the whole world knowing her private business.

'So, you've really started, then,' I said, trying to make a better job than last time of hiding my envy.

'It seems that way,' Frankie replied.

'So what's it like?' I asked.

Frankie shrugged and changed the subject. There was no one sitting anywhere near us, but she wouldn't talk about it until we'd paid for our drinks and were out of Alf Resco's, walking down to the lower ferry, which would take her over to Kingswear.

We stopped on the quay where the cars queue up, watching the ferry with its little tug working its way towards us. Here Frankie confided that the blood wasn't coming monthly, like she'd been led to believe, but only when she peed, and that she had an ache which hardly ever went away.

'It's really horrible,' she said. 'Sometimes I think I can't live like this. I feel really depressed. I keep taking Mummy's paracetamol and I'm worried that she'll notice.'

It certainly sounded horrible. I remember staring across the water at the brightly coloured houses on Kingswear Hill, feeling glad, after all, that I hadn't started my own periods. Frankie should tell her mother, I advised, and she agreed. But I could tell from her voice that she wouldn't do it.

The ferry arrived and cars drove off it and other cars drove on. Just before Frankie walked down the ramp to join them, she dug deep in her school bag and said that, before she forgot, she had a present for me.

It was her old mobile phone. Up until that time I hadn't had one of my own and all our arrangements to meet had been done in school by email. Now, however, Frankie had a new phone and her old one, complete with about twenty pounds' worth of credit, was going begging.

That night I phoned her for the first time. I remember how excited I felt and how grown up as well. We talked about all sorts of silly things, just because we could. Then, in the dark, with nobody around to hear us, I brought up the subject of periods again. What did Frankie mean about pain? How bad was it? Did it ever go away? And the blood that came out in her pee – what was it like? Was it normal blood?

'I don't know,' said Frankie. 'What's normal for a period?'

'You should ask your mother, not me,' I said.

Frankie laughed at that. Would I talk to *my* mother about periods, she said. And the answer, of course, was no.

'What about one of your school friends?' I said. 'Or your teachers. Or you must have a school first-aid person, or nurse, or someone like that.'

'You're fussing. Stop it. There's really nothing wrong. This is just what periods are like. I wish I'd never mentioned it,' Frankie said.

I knew that I was fussing, but next time Frankie and I spoke on the phone I couldn't resist having another go. This time she got really mad at me and said that I was prying. But she did admit that the blood thing was still happening, and so were the pains.

When I got off the phone, I plucked up my courage and asked Mum what to do about period pains if they got really bad. I refused to give the name of the friend whose condition I was describing, which was a mistake, because she thought it was me. Before I was even halfway through going on about blood in pee, she was racing round the house looking for sanitary towels, as if it had never occurred to her that one day her daughter might grow up.

Eventually Mum found some and put them in a brown paper bag, giving them to me as if they were some terrible secret. She said I was to make sure I never ran out and, if I got blood on my knickers, I was to rinse them in cold water before washing them with soap. Also, if the pain got too bad, hot-water bottles always helped.

All the way through, I tried saying that I wasn't asking for myself. But either Mum didn't believe me or she didn't hear, too busy going on about how sad it was that little girls had to grow up.

In the end, it was Grandma who sorted me out. The house on Clarence Street was Grandma's kingdom, which she ruled through the party wall. No one could get away with anything without her knowing about it. No one could have a private conversation. Even in our side of the house, with the telly on or the radio, Grandma somehow managed to hear what people were saying.

We all hated it, but there was nothing we could do. Mum complained that she hated living in Grandma's house anyway, which she reckoned was like Doctor Who's Tardis in reverse – big on the outside but tiny when you got through the door. But Dad always refused to move. He was Grandma's one and only baby and she had him wrapped round her little finger. No way, he said, could his mother live on her own. And, besides, did we know how much houses cost in Dartmouth? We couldn't afford to live anywhere else.

No sooner had Mum whizzed off to recover from the shock of having a daughter old enough for periods than Grandma emerged through one of the doors, declaring that if *her* friend had blood in her pee, she'd make her see a doctor pronto.

'You should phone your friend back,' she said, 'and tell her so. If you don't, you might regret it, and life's too short for regrets.'

Gladys

One night, some time after telling Frankie that, according to my grandmother, she'd got to see a doctor, I was summoned up to Bradley Castle. It was the early hours of the morning, long after the ferry had closed down, but Frankie informed me that I had to come now.

'You mean straight away?' I said. 'Tonight?'

'What's wrong with that?' Frankie replied.

What was wrong was that my parents would kill me. Rambling round the town by day was one thing, but doing it by night was another. And I wasn't sure I wanted to visit Bradley Castle anyway and have Frankie's wealthy lifestyle rubbed in my face. Besides, there was a little matter of the River Dart, which lay between us.

'The ferry stopped running hours ago,' I said.

'Well, borrow a boat, then,' Frankie replied. 'What does everybody else do?'

This was true. When the Dartmouth and Kingswear pubs close at night it's a common occurrence for people to 'borrow' boats to get themselves back home. It happens all the time. Any boat with oars in, or a working motor, is considered fair game.

But *I'd* never done it. Nor had I been on the river in the dark, let alone on my own. And I'm not exactly what you'd call one of life's risk-takers. I tried explaining this to Frankie, but she got cross. What sort of friend was I? She'd never asked for anything before. Besides, where was my spirit of adventure?

It was on the tip of my tongue to say that I didn't have a spirit of adventure, never had done and never would. But there was something strange in Frankie's voice that couldn't be ignored. So I got up, dressed, sneaked down to the boat-float, grabbed the first small craft with a working outboard motor and headed out across the water, promising I'd bring it back. My heart was hammering but, looking back, it wasn't fear that drove it. It was the sense that trouble was waiting for me on the other shore.

If I could ever get to it, that was. The River Dart is faster than it sometimes looks and its currents are much stronger. I'd crossed it plenty of times before, but never on my own, and that night it took far longer than I'd expected. I was exhausted when I came ashore in Kingswear. To make matters worse, I'd ended up at the wrong landing point, which meant that the walk up the hill to Frankie's house took twice as long as it should have done.

There'd better be a good reason for me doing this, I thought as I trudged up a succession of connecting footpaths and alleys, without a clue where I was heading.

Eventually, after a couple of wrong turns, I came out on top of Kingswear Hill and found myself facing a high, protective wall and electric gate, behind which lay the roofs and chimneys of Bradley Castle. The gate was closed and the notice on it informed me that guard dogs were on the prowl.

I texted Frankie, worried that after all the time I'd taken she might be asleep. Much to my relief, however, she texted straight back.

'Stay where you are,' she said. 'I'll be right down.'

Two minutes later, Frankie appeared at the gate, which she opened carefully so that no one would hear it clanging. I wasn't to worry about the dogs, she said, because the notice was there to deter burglars and the dogs didn't exist.

We crossed the terrace and entered the house through the French windows of a room she called 'the Snug', which had a high ceiling, a huge old fireplace, lots of books, heavy carved-oak furniture and didn't look very snug to me. I'd have been perfectly happy to go no further, but Frankie insisted on dragging me up and down a series of staircases and half landings until we reached her bedroom.

Here I found myself confronted by enough space to comfortably accommodate our side of Grandma's house. Frankie's bedroom looked like something in a film set. It was full of white rugs, sinking sofas, flat-screen TV and computer screens, walls full of books and CDs, a massive music centre, silver-framed photographs of Frankie swimming, riding, wind-surfing and playing tennis, wardrobes with mirror doors and a four-poster bed swathed in baby-blue net.

I felt as if I'd walked into a dream. There were enormous fluffy teddy bears everywhere and tropical plants with huge leaves. A heavily panelled door with an ornate cut-glass handle led to the biggest bathroom I'd ever seen, tiled in silver and blue, with a shower, sunken bath, full-length mirror and stacks of fluffy towels. Next to the bathroom, doors opened onto a balcony which overlooked the most incredible view.

I went and stood out there, and could have stayed forever, looking out across the river to the castle and the sea. But Frankie dragged me back in again and closed the door behind us. She drew the curtains, which were silver and blue and matched everything else, even her hairbrushes and the pens and note-paper on her desk.

Even Frankie's dressing gown and slippers were silver and blue. I felt as if, simply by standing there in my uncoordinated clothes, I was spoiling the effect. I remember wishing I hadn't come. We'd always been equals down in Castle Cove. But here the dif-ference between us was inescapable.

'I want to talk to you,' Frankie said nervously, almost formally. 'Thank you for coming. Shall we sit down?'

Again there was that something in her voice. But now there was something in Frankie's face as well – something tight and shiny that I'd never seen before, as if some secret was about to come spilling out.

'What is it?' I said, sitting gingerly on the edge of her bed. 'There had better be a good reason for dragging me all this way.'

I was trying to make light of things, but Frankie was in deadly earnest. She sat down too. Usually she wasn't the sort of person who was lost for words, but this time she seemed not to know where to start. For a moment the two of us stared at each other. Then suddenly it all came out – a stream of information about going to the doctor like I'd said, and being right to tell her to talk to her mother, and tests, and being frightened, and going for results.

When she began, I couldn't for a minute figure out what she was on about. It wasn't that I'd forgotten about the blood in her pee, but it took me a while to make the right connections.

'What tests?' I said.

'The ones I've just got the results from,' Frankie said.

'Tests to decide if you've started having periods?' I said, struggling to understand what she was telling me

'Yes, if you like,' Frankie replied, exasperation in her voice. 'Except that I haven't. We got that wrong. And I've got to have an operation and I've never had one before. I mean, I've never had *anything* before, and I don't know what to expect. Charis, I know this probably sounds stupid, but I'm really scared.'

Frankie looked at me with huge eyes. She wasn't the sort of person to ever be scared about anything, but then she wasn't the sort of person to have an operation either. She was the fittest, healthiest person I'd ever met.

'I don't understand,' I said.

'I don't either,' Frankie replied. 'Apparently it's my kidneys that are to blame. Except I don't even know where my kidneys are. The doctor drew a diagram, but I've forgotten already where everything was.'

She looked at me as if I might be able to help. But she was looking at the wrong person. I'd always been hopeless at human biology in school. Hopeless at all the sciences, especially where diagrams were involved. I was a dreamer. I was no good at real life. My mind was full of make-believe, and physical things like bodies and what went on in them, and graphs and diagrams and things like that, were a mystery to me.

Frankie started on about 'irregularities' – something to do with bleeding and the reason for her niggling pain. It was only when I caught the word *growth* that I began to catch her general drift.

'What sort of growth?' I demanded to know.

Frankie shrugged. 'A growth's a growth, isn't it?' she said.

'How big is this growth?' I said.

'I don't know,' she replied.

'What do you mean, you *don't know*?'

'*I DON'T KNOW.* Honestly, Charis – next you'll be asking me if it's got a name. Which I suppose it always could have, if you want. We could call it Gladys if you like. But the name the doctor gave it is cancer, just in case you're wondering.'

Cancer. The word sliced through me like a knife, but I remember saying calmly, as if a bomb hadn't just gone off in both our lives, 'Oh well, at least you know what the problem is.'

'I suppose I do,' Frankie agreed.

'Except that I always thought only old people got cancer.'

'So did I.'

We stared at each other helplessly. Frankie said that apparently this problem in her kidneys had lain dormant for years, which was very rare indeed. But at least they'd finally located it, and that was what mattered, according to the consultant.

I remember being stunned into silence. Frankie, on the other hand, having got the thing out, couldn't stop talking about it. The idea of something hidden inside her for all those years completely spooked her, she said. That was why she'd asked me up. Why it couldn't wait until next time we met. Couldn't even wait until morning.

'I feel as if I don't know myself any more,' she said. 'What else lies in there, that I never knew about? I want to tear myself open just to check that everything else is all right. But I can't, of course. And, besides, I wouldn't know where to start.'

I sat there nodding, feeling helpless. I wanted there to be something useful I could do, but I couldn't think what. Frankie ran out of things to say and, for a moment, silence hung between us. Then I asked when the operation would take place and

Frankie said, 'The day after tomorrow.'

'*The day after tomorrow?*' I repeated.

Frankie gave me a thin smile. 'Now they know what's wrong, they want to deal with it,' she said. 'But I'm not to worry, because I'm young and strong, and the Royal South Hams has a very good track record on this sort of thing. Apparently.'

She sighed and made the strangest little fluttering gesture with her hands. She looked so lost, and suddenly it came to me that there *was* something I could do. Maybe we'd never been ones for hugs and kisses, like some of her flamingo friends, but I put my arms round her and we held each other tight.

Frankie's Flying Dream

When Frankie was small, she had a flying dream. It only happened once, but she remembered it ever after. In it she was caught up by a strange white wind that looked like rain, but wasn't wet and shone like silk. It got her in its grip but, instead of making her its prisoner, it made her feel incredibly free. It carried her over the top of her house, over the cliffs, over the sea and finally to an island far away where, on a high hill with steep green sides, it totally pinned her down and yet she still felt free.

'It was the most wonderful moment,' Frankie said. 'Beyond what I could ever describe. Even pinned down on that hillside, I could still feel myself flying. I wasn't imagining it. I knew I was really doing it. I was wholly and completely pinned to that hill, and yet another part of me – which felt whole and complete too – was flying high above me and making me feel free.'

Frankie said the experience had been so strange and wonderful that it had made her laugh. She'd still been laughing when she awoke and, after that, laughter, flight and freedom had always been connected in her mind.

'The only person I've ever told this to is you,' she said. 'I've always thought it would be impossible to explain and, anyway, that no one would understand.'

I was flattered. I wasn't sure that I *did* understand, but no way would I have admitted it. I was terrified of flying. Hated planes. Hoped I'd never have to go on one. As far as I was concerned, any dream of flight would have been a nightmare.

Frankie, on the other hand, wanted nothing more in life. When she grew up she even dreamt of making a career out of flying. Her father wanted her to become a lawyer, but she went on so much about becoming a pilot that one day he even arranged for her to take the controls of a friend's plane.

Frankie got really excited about that. In fact, we both did, even though I wasn't going and it's the last thing I'd have wanted to do anyway. I remember us beforehand, down in Castle Cove, talking about what it was going to be like. Frankie was convinced that the pilot of the plane would say, *You're a natural*

– *you should make flying your career*, and then her father would forget all about law school and send her to some sort of pilots' school instead.

On the great day, however, things didn't turn out the way Frankie had expected. Maybe she'd hoped for too much and reality couldn't match up. Or maybe flying simply wasn't like that and her dream had misled her.

But, either way, when Frankie took the controls she said it didn't feel like flying at all. She didn't feel in charge, no matter what the pilot said about her doing it. Sitting before all those buttons, lights and bleeping noises, there was none of the freedom she'd been looking for – nothing to make her laugh, not even anything to make her scared.

'It was weird,' Frankie said. 'I didn't really feel like I was up in the air. Everything around me felt so, I don't know, so *solid*, I suppose.'

For a while after that, Frankie went quiet on the flying front. Other interests took over and it was forgotten. Only when she went into the Royal South Hams Hospital did she mention it again.

It was the night before the operation and she was calling from her private room, even though it was against hospital rules to use her mobile phone. I'd have thought that flying would be the last thing on her mind, but suddenly, right out of the blue,

Frankie asked if I could fix it up for her when she came out of hospital.

'What do you mean?' I said, not quite grasping what she wanted. 'Fix up what exactly? What have you got in mind?'

Frankie said she didn't know. Hang-gliding, paragliding, sky-diving, even piloting a plane again – I could take my pick. But what she wanted, she said, was something to look forward to after her operation. Something to face tomorrow with. The knowledge of good things to come, and there was no way her father was going to fix it up – not after she'd been ill like this.

'So fix it up for me,' she said.

'What . . . how . . . why?' I spluttered.

'Why have you always got to question everything?' Frankie said. 'It's obvious, isn't it? *Just get me flying*. That's all I ask.'

Book Two

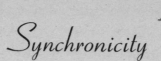

Synchronicity

In an extraordinary example of what my brother Damo – who has a theory on the subject – calls synchronicity, both Frankie's parents and mine had massive rows during the time she was in hospital. Frankie's parents' one was about how she should be treated when she'd recovered from her operation, and it happened at her bedside, of all places. But my parents' row took place at home on Clarence Street, while I was upstairs revising for my end-of-year tests.

It was about the garden, which had always been my grandad's pride and joy and, before he died, had apparently been a picture, right the way from the lawns and flower-bed, to the vegetable garden and the disused pigpen. Dad hated gardening, which meant that everything now lay neglected. He hated soil, Dad said. He hated weeds. He hated the way that half the time the things you were trying to cultivate never came up. In fact, as far as Dad was concerned, all gardens should be covered in decking and all flowers and shrubs restricted to pots.

But Grandma wanted her garden kept up, which meant that there were continual rows between her and Dad about Grandad's flowers going to seed, his pond drying up, his herb garden being forgotten, his box hedges being uncut and his apple trees, no longer pruned, failing to bear fruit.

These were all Dad's fault. He had let them go. It wasn't Grandma's job to do the gardening, it was his.

So one day when Dad came in from the Cherub – where he goes to drink sometimes to get away from being nagged – announcing that he'd found a gardener, he expected everyone to be as delighted as him. He even invited Grandma in to share the news. Apparently some friendly widow called Judith Mason had offered to come round and sort out the garden. For free.

'So, what do you think of that?' Dad said.

'No one does anything for free,' Mum replied, looking surprised. 'She must want something.'

'Perhaps you've found yourself a girlfriend,' Damo cracked.

Everybody laughed, except for Mum, who, with

her typical wariness of anybody new, said that she thought the whole thing sounded highly suspicious.

'This Judith Mason person is offering to sort out the garden for free, is she?' she said. 'For no more reason than out of the goodness of her heart? Nobody nowadays does anything out of the goodness of their heart. And especially if they don't know you. So who is she? I've never heard of her. She could be anybody. You can never be too careful these days. No way am I having some stranger hanging round my garden.'

Grandma – who was as keen as Dad to get the garden sorted out – pointed out that it was hers, not Mum's. At this, Mum's face flushed with anger and I slipped upstairs. I could see the direction things were taking. And I was right too. Before I'd even reached my bedroom I could hear Mum's voice rising, followed by Dad's and Grandma's. I closed the door behind me, got out my revision books and tried to focus on something else. But it was impossible. Even up in the attic, I could hear what was going on.

First Mum insisted, yet again, that something sinister was going on. Then Dad said that, to the contrary, Judith Mason was a godsend. Then Mum said that Damo was right when he talked about girlfriends and that this Judith Mason person was flirting with Dad. Then everybody laughed.

But Mum wasn't joking. 'There's more to this than gardening,' I heard her crying out. 'So don't laugh at me like I'm a fool. And don't think you can weasel some woman into your life and I won't notice. Damo's right. This Judith Mason person's got a thing for you. *That's* what this is all about.'

I crept out onto the landing and stood at the top of the stairs, looking down into the living room. No way could I get any revision done. I could see Damo's back, Grandma's feet in their slippers and Mum striding up and down. I couldn't see Dad, but I could hear him spluttering at the thought of anybody fancying him, or him fancying them.

'Judith Mason might be available,' he said, 'in that she's a widow. But she's also middle-aged and dumpy. Not my type at all. I like my girls with a bit of spark. As you should know . . .'

He came across the room and tried to hug Mum. But she wasn't having any of it and pushed him away. Grandma left, saying that she'd had enough. I heard the door bang between her side of the house and ours. Then Damo said he'd had enough as well and headed off down to the pub.

'There. See what you've done,' Mum said. 'You've driven everybody away. First Charis, then your mother and now even Damo. This is all your fault.'

'*Mine?*' Dad said, his voice rising to a dangerous pitch.

Before I could hear what happened next, Frankie texted me an SOS: 'Parents rowing. Text me. HELP!' All too willingly, I retreated to my bedroom, closed the door and climbed onto the high window ledge, where my reception was always best. Here I texted back that my parents were rowing too.

'You wouldn't believe the noise they're making,' I spelt out.

'I believe you,' Frankie spelt back.

Frankie's parents' row had nothing to do with anybody fancying anybody else, but everything to do with blame. After hours on the Internet, Mr Bradley had come to the conclusion that Frankie's condition was genetic – and that it came from her mother's side of the family. Hardly surprisingly, Mrs Bradley was furious, claiming that cigar smoke had done the damage, which she'd been forced to inhale against her will right through her pregnancies, and it was lucky they didn't all have cancer, given how much Mr Bradley smoked.

Mr Bradley retorted that the problem just as likely came from Mrs Bradley's obsession with ready meals, which she was always buying in bulk, too lazy to cook for herself although she had a state-of-the-art kitchen.

'Everybody knows that meals like that, packed full of preservatives, give you cancer,' he said.

'And everybody knows that cancer comes from mobile phones,' Frankie's mother said. 'So why you bought Frankie one, and encourage her to be on it all the time by paying for her calls, I simply don't know.'

By now, Frankie informed me, she lay forgotten between them in her hospital bed, the object of an argument instead of a real live person recovering from an operation. According to her parents, everything was suddenly carcinogenic, from the dye in her hair to the chemicals in her bedroom furniture.

'THIS IS AWFUL,' Frankie texted. 'I can't believe what's going on. The whole hospital must be able to hear it. It's SO embarrassing. I want to DIE.'

I wanted to die too. I texted back, saying never mind her and her hospital ward, our entire street, including Bryony Rogers, my mortal enemy, who lived two doors down, could hear what my parents were shouting at each other.

'Parents!' we both agreed.

Frankie came home a couple of days later, and I was there to witness her return, positioned outside the gate of Bradley Castle under a huge old beech tree where no one but she would notice me. Her father's car came up the hill, with Frankie sitting in the back propped up with cushions like visiting royalty. The electric gates flew open and she went sweeping through. Before the gates closed again, I saw the car draw to a halt and her parents go round to lift her out as if she was a sick dog back from the vet.

It came as a shock to see how incapable she was. Only a short time ago Frankie had been swimming, sailing and larking about in Castle Cove. Now, from the way her parents flapped around her, it seemed she wasn't even capable of taking a step.

For an hour after that, I lurked about in the wood opposite the house, which was on slightly higher ground, allowing me a view of cars coming and going, bringing nurses, Frankie's brothers, her best friends from school, the neighbours and several deliveries of flowers. The stream of people was endless. How Frankie put up with all those visitors, I really don't know. I texted and, hardly surprisingly, got no reply except a message later on saying that she was fine.

After that, I didn't hear again for a while. I couldn't afford to phone because I'd run out of credit, so I sent a series of emails from school. I didn't hear back, though, and in the meantime I had end-of-year tests to take up my attention, plus the extraordinary makeover of Grandma's garden by Judith Mason.

She arrived one afternoon, complete with tools. I came home from the first of my tests and there she was – short, stumpy, smiling, her sandy-coloured hair tied back with a twist of scarf, her green eyes shining and her face bright red from the exertion of tackling our wilderness.

She waved as I shut the street door behind me and came up the steps. I pretended I hadn't noticed. I'd never met this woman before and no way was I going to acknowledge her as if we were friends. On any other occasion, I might have done my day's revision in the garden, but I went inside and slammed the door behind me out of loyalty to Mum.

Judith Mason remained out in the garden until it was too dark to see properly. When Mum came home from work, she was still at it, pulling up weeds and hacking back the undergrowth. Mum didn't offer her any supper and Dad wouldn't have dared. Not even Grandma dared. But, by the time Judith Mason left that night, the garden had been returned to its old shape and all sorts of plants had emerged that we hadn't seen since Grandad's days.

Grandma was thrilled and so was Dad. Judith Mason was a marvel, they both agreed. In one day alone she'd achieved more than Dad had ever done.

'Come again,' he said as his new best friend left. 'Any time. You're always welcome. You know where we are.'

Judith Mason laughed at that and said perhaps she would. 'You've got a lovely garden here. Quite the hidden treasure,' she said.

Dad beamed as if he couldn't have been more flattered if she'd said it about him personally. 'We'd even pay you,' he said – which was something coming from him.

'I wouldn't dream of it,' Judith Mason replied. 'The only way I'd come back is for love. A garden like this deserves nothing less.'

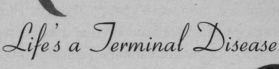

Life's a Terminal Disease

Frankie phoned one night, right out of the blue. It was after I'd finished the last of my end-of-year tests, when school didn't seem worth bothering with any more and the summer holidays were close but not close enough. I awoke in the darkness to the sound of my phone buzzing in my school bag, scrambled to reach it and only just got there in time.

'What was keeping you?' Frankie said.

'Good to hear from you too,' I replied. 'If you must know, I was asleep.'

'Sleeping's for wimps,' Frankie said. 'The moon's out and it's a perfect night for crossing the river. Why don't you come up to my place?'

'Is something wrong?' I asked, remembering last time.

'Why should anything be wrong?' Frankie replied. She sounded light and cheerful but, even so, I could have sworn there was an edge to her voice.

I got dressed, but I wasn't happy about it. The last time Frankie had wanted me to cross the river it was because she'd discovered she had cancer, I thought as I dressed, sneaked out of the house and padded down through the shadows to the boat-float. So what could be up this time?

Praying that I'd got it all wrong, I 'borrowed' another boat and crossed to Kingswear. It was hard going, because the tide was high and running against me. At one point I thought I wouldn't make it and almost turned back.

But my fear that there just might be something wrong kept me going. What if Frankie hadn't just asked me up for a bit of fun, and some deadly purpose lay behind her request? No way could I turn back.

Finally, with the sound of St Petrox's bells ringing out across the water, I arrived at Frankie's gate. I remember listening to them as I stood outside the gate, texting Frankie to say that I was there. She came down and let me in. Immediately I was certain that I'd been right to come. Frankie's expression was grave. Something was definitely up.

In silence, she led me across the terrace, through the French windows and up to her room. Only when the door was shut and the two of us faced each other in the darkness did she finally speak. Her eyes were huge. All around her I could smell flowers and see the shapes of get-well cards.

'Do you know that cancer's a word, not a sentence?' she announced.

'Do I know *what*?' I replied.

'And life's a terminal disease,' she said.

'I'm sorry?' I said.

'Did you know that if anyone can beat this thing it's me?' Frankie said. 'It's important to *think positive*. Did you know that? And to *take control of my life*. And to *always look on the bright side*. Did you know that if it's not *one thing, it's another* and life's a *vale of tears* but we've got to *rise above it*. Sometimes we've got to *get back in the driving seat* and *face our demons* and *bite the bullet*. We've got to *laugh in the face of everything life throws at us*. And that's why you're here – so that you can laugh with me . . .'

Suddenly Frankie switched on the light and lunged at me with a pillow. Her eyes were sparkling with a merriment that caught me off guard. 'Laugh, damn you, laugh!' she cried as I held up my arms, trying to protect myself. The grave tone had gone and she was pounding me, while at the same time laughing her head off about every last thing that anybody had said.

'God, Frankie!' I cried out. 'I thought something terrible had happened. I hate you – I swear I do! You nearly scared me to death.'

Frankie laughed, and hit all the harder. 'All that's happened,' she said, 'is that a little lump's been removed. And yet I've got all these cards full of terrible advice and people keep phoning up with more of it. It's like a funeral parlour round here. And it's been like this ever since I got back. It's driving me crazy.'

'So you thought you'd drive me crazy too, did you?' I said.

I grabbed another pillow and started beating her back. She had no excuse, I said, for worrying me half silly. *Whack! Thwack!* 'I thought that you were dying,' I said. *Punch! Thud!*

'I know you did,' Frankie replied, thwacking me even harder. 'And so, it seems, does everybody else. You've got to see the funny side.'

I *did* see the funny side, but that didn't stop me beating Frankie until she begged for mercy.

'Oh, it's so good to see you again!' she cried when neither of us could stand straight any more and her entire bedroom was a mass of feathers.

'Good to see you too!' I said.

'It's been terrible round here,' Frankie said. 'What I really want is to go back to school, now that my operation's over. And the doctors say I'm better and it would be good for me, but my parents won't allow it. I'm not strong enough, they say. They're continually telling me to think positive, but every time I try to put that into practice, they call me a poor, dear girl and tell me to rest.'

I said that *a poor, dear girl* was nothing compared to what Frankie would become if she ever put me through this again. She said it had been worth it just to see my face. Then she promised to come down to Castle Cove the following weekend, to make it up to me.

'But your parents won't let you out,' I said.

'I know they won't,' Frankie agreed. 'But I'll still be there. You wait and see.'

The following day, I went down after school to get Castle Cove to ready for Frankie's return. The den was in particular need of attention, having fallen foul of a series of exceptionally high tides. Some of the furniture had been washed away, while a ton and a half of seaweed had been deposited in the throne room.

I made everything safe again, refixing all the planks and pallets that had worked themselves loose. Then I cleared out the rubbish that the tide had brought in and redecorated throughout. I wanted everything to be perfect for Frankie's return. But the next time I saw her wasn't down in Castle Cove, as I'd hoped.

She phoned to say she hadn't been able to arrange it, after all, and could we meet for a quick drink in Alf Resco's instead. When I arrived, I found my milkshake waiting for me, paid for already, and Frankie in a very different mood from the one she'd been in the other night. There was nothing to laugh about this time. Rather, she seemed angry and distracted.

I might have been a blank wall as far as she was concerned, not her old friend Charis Watts. No sooner had I sat down than she launched into me as if she had things to say and had to say them fast. Did I know, she told me, that her parents had been to the Royal South Hams to meet her doctors *behind her back*? They went to talk about her, but they didn't even think to invite her.

I said how weird that was. Frankie said it wasn't half as weird as the way they'd behaved when they returned home.

'Mummy was really angry,' she said, 'but wouldn't explain why. And Daddy was going on about us moving to the US, where the medical profession knew what it was talking about – whatever *that* meant. Mummy said over her dead body were we moving at a time like this. I asked what *a time like this* meant, but she didn't seem to hear. Neither of them did. They were too busy shouting at each other.

'Mummy was going on about complementary medical treatments that she'd read about – acupuncture, crystal therapy and things like that – and Daddy was going on about her being stupid. He even went so far as to say he wished he'd never married her. *It was the mistake of my life*, he said. After that, there was no stopping them, both accusing the other of only thinking of themselves – but the one they really weren't thinking of was me.

'I kept on asking what was wrong, but nobody answered. It was as if I wasn't there. Daddy said no way was he having his daughter surrounded by nutty crystal therapists. Mummy said that Daddy had the most closed mind she'd ever met. Then Daddy got really mad and said, *I mean it, Di. If you try and come between our daughter and proper treatment, I'll divorce you and take custody.*'

'What proper treatment?' I said, feeling a chill wind blowing through me. Frankie was better – wasn't she?

She looked at me with irritation, as if I'd missed the point. 'Never mind the treatment,' she said, waving a hand dismissively. 'Haven't you been listening? I'm talking about my parents *getting a divorce*! I mean, how terrible is that? I don't know what's the matter with them. They've always been so happy. And that's what life is all about, isn't it? What more could anybody want?'

By this time the whole of Alf Resco's was listening in, from the tables down by the entrance where the tourists congregate, to the ones at the back, underneath the rambling vines, where the locals tend to sit. Frankie noticed and turned bright red. She buried herself in her milkshake, sucking noisily through her straw. Unable to wait for her to finish, I leant across and asked again about the treatment.

'I thought that you were better,' I said. 'So what's this all about? I don't understand.'

Maybe Frankie didn't understand either. Certainly she wasn't going to stop and explain. All she wanted to talk about was her parents. Chemotherapy, radiotherapy or whatever it was that her doctors were recommending counted for nothing.

We finished our milkshakes and went outside. From Alf Resco's it's only a short walk down to the lower ferry, where Frankie said her mother would be waiting. She turned to go, but I pulled her back.

'Are you telling me you've still got, you know – *cancer*?' I said.

But Frankie wouldn't tell me anything. 'Mummy's waiting. I've got to go. I can't hang about. We'll speak later. *Byeee* . . .' she said.

On Friendship

Frankie went home and I went down to my beautifully spring-cleaned Castle Cove and sat wondering what had hit me. In fact, that's where I am now, all these years later, writing in my notebook under the tree where we had our den, watching kids paddling in what used to be our private waters, thinking about friendship and how much it means.

That other evening, I remember trailing home for supper, thinking that if anything happened to Frankie I'd be alone in the world without a single friend. As if to prove how bleak that would be, I bumped into Bryony Rogers at the top of Clarence Street, who came rushing over when she saw me. Normally Bryony treated me as if I was beneath contempt, but today she obviously had information she wanted to get out of me.

'What's this I hear about Frankie Bradley?' she said before I could sidle past her and get home.

'I don't know what you're talking about,' I replied.

Bryony rolled her eyes. 'You can't fool me,' she said. 'You're her friend. I know you are. My mother saw you in Alf Resco's.'

I said her mother must have mistaken me for someone else, and why would a girl like Frankie Bradley want to be friends with me?

Bryony agreed. 'That's exactly what I said to Mum,' she said. 'I said she must have mixed you up with someone else. No one in their right mind would be friends with you. But you'd better not be lying. No one lies to me if they want to stay alive.'

Bryony took a step towards me, full of menace, as if to illustrate what she meant. But Mum suddenly appeared, as if she'd heard our voices and knew I needed help.

'What's going on?' she said, fixing Bryony with her steely eyes.

Bryony sloped away. She didn't like my mum.

'I'd be getting along, if I were you,' Mum called after her, and stood on the road, with her hands on her hips, making sure that she did.

Wind of Change

Perhaps now's the time to write about Mum. She's a good old mum, but nobody would describe her as easy. She's shy for starters, which sometimes makes her abrupt, and she finds it hard to make friends, and some people think she's tactless because she says what she thinks. But she's kind as well, and means no harm, and she has talents that most people never get to know about.

Take her singing, for example. Dad always reckoned Mum could have been a pop star if she'd wanted, because her voice is that good. But she hates pop. It's opera that she loves. She'll sing it in the bath when she thinks no one's about. She'll sing it anywhere – and yet none of us expected her to go and join a choir. But that's what she did.

It was the choir that met to practise in the big town church, and Mum even managed to become one of its soloists. I remember the first time I heard her singing with them. Dad and Damo were there as well and we nearly died of shock. The choir was dressed in uniform, all the same in black and white, but even so Mum stood out. Most of what she sang was classical – Mozart, Handel and things like that. But one piece was a tricky modern thing that obviously hadn't been composed for novices, and yet she got it off note-perfect and the review in the *Dartmouth Herald Express* mentioned her by name.

For a while after that, Mum was a bit of a star around Dartmouth. The choir was in demand and it was all because of her. People would stop her on the street to thank her for singing. Mum would blush and hurry away, but you could tell that she was pleased.

One day, however, the old choirmaster retired and a younger man took over. He ditched the boring black and white uniform and tried to do the same with much of the music. Old-fashioned songs were out and modern ones were in. Likewise opera in favour of pop.

It was the end of the choir, as far as Mum was concerned, and the end of her singing career. Most of the choir went along with the new music, but a few walked out, and Mum was one of them.

After that, she stayed at home and sulked. The choir recruited new people and the bright young choirmaster became the talk of Dartmouth. A wind of change was in the air. Some people said about time too, but Mum wasn't one of them.

The town was full of newcomers and she didn't like it. Suddenly they were everywhere, it seemed. Like that Judith Mason woman. Taking over choirs. Doing other people's gardening. Acting like they owned the place.

Strangely enough, someone who agreed with Mum was Mrs Bradley. Not long after the concert that Dad, Damo and I went to, she joined the choir as well, and later she became one of the people who walked out, incensed at ditching the 'Hallelujah Chorus' for Kylie Minogue's 'I Should Be So Lucky'.

I'd have thought Mrs Bradley would have liked Kylie Minogue, but apparently not. Not that I knew that then, or found out until much later. If Frankie knew about her mother and the choir, she certainly never let on. But then her mind was full of other things. Like her parents' supposed divorce and her father's plans to send her abroad for treatment.

Neither of those things actually ever happened, but that didn't stop the Dartmouth rumours. Frankie had cancer, everybody knew that. She'd had an operation, but the whole world knew it hadn't done the trick. Now, according to Dartmouth, all sorts of treatments were on the books – not just chemotherapy, but new wonder drugs, lasers, key-hole surgery, you name it.

Damo came home from the boats one day having heard that Frankie's treatment was costing so much that her parents were being forced to sell Bradley Castle. I relayed this back to Frankie and we both had a good laugh. Another time he said that she was going to Cape Town for treatment and we laughed about that too.

For the truth was that, after a massive battle between Frankie's parents, the chemotherapy department at the Royal South Hams, here in Devon, had won the day. Some local cancer expert known to Frankie's mother had informed them that Dr Herbert of the Royal South Hams was a world-class specialist in his field. They'd been to see him. Mr Bradley had been won round. And Frankie had even gone so far as to fall in love with him.

His name was Eustace, which Frankie, blinded by love, reckoned was a wonderful name. He was a million times more handsome than anybody she had ever fancied before, including Orlando Bloom, who was by now definitely last year's news. Why anyone would want to go halfway round the world to be treated by anybody else, she couldn't imagine. She'd be safe with Dr Herbert. In fact, she couldn't wait for him to get his hands on her.

Looking on the Bright Side

The day before Frankie started her chemotherapy treatment, she and I sneaked down to Castle Cove. We only had a short time together, so we had to make the most of it. Hangliness was banned and laftishness was the order of the day. Sitting in our den with the sea glistening before us, every moment felt important. I remember Frankie's hair blowing across her face like a sheet of crumpled silk. And yet, an hour later she was in the hairdresser's and it was on the floor.

Having it cut off was something that Dr Herbert had suggested as a means of helping Frankie come to terms with the consequences of her treatment. Her mother hadn't wanted her to do it, but he'd reckoned it might make her feel more in control, and Frankie had agreed with him.

How anybody takes a decision like that, I've no idea. Afterwards, Frankie texted me a photo so that

I'd recognise her, she said, next time we met. But I knew what she looked like anyway. When she'd come out of the hairdresser's, I'd been across the road. I'd seen her and her mother go in, and seen them come out again, Frankie with her pink, shorn head.

'What do you think?' said Frankie's text.

I texted back that I thought she looked sensational – more like a supermodel than a chemotherapy patient – and more people should shave their heads. We agreed she'd phone me the following evening after her first treatment. We also agreed that I'd be outside her house next morning, to see her off.

I was there bright and early, waiting in the shadow of my usual old beech tree, my eyes fixed on the electric gate, which was already open. It took a while for Frankie to appear. First I saw her mother packing out the car with cushions and magazines. Then George and Diggers came out, checking their watches as if they were their sister's minders.

Then, finally, Frankie appeared on her father's arm. Yesterday she'd been fine, but the way her family behaved around her, you'd have thought she was incapable of walking on her own. Everybody gathered round protectively to help her into the car. Her mother sat on one side of her and Diggers on the other, then her father and George got into the front. The car pulled out of the drive and the gates closed behind it. It turned down the hill and, for a moment, I thought Frankie hadn't seen me.

But, just as she was whisked away, Frankie turned her head and looked out of the back window. She knew where I was. Our eyes didn't exactly meet, but I knew my presence had been registered and raised a hand as if to say *good luck*. Then Frankie was gone.

That night, when she was back home again, she phoned as promised, but there wasn't much to tell. Chemotherapy hadn't been much fun, she said, but at least there'd never be another first day and she was one treatment closer to it being over. After the next session she phoned as well. Again there wasn't much to say, but the next time she phoned she complained of tiredness and said she felt sick.

After that, we didn't speak for ages. Frankie texted a few times, but then the texts dried up and, whenever I tried to phone, her mobile was always off. I kept on texting, though, sending little messages saying things like *Thinking of you*. But Frankie never replied. It was as if she was a princess in a tower who'd shut herself off from the outside world by pulling up the drawbridge.

Why she did that, I've no idea. Other chemotherapy patients I've heard of since live normal lives, see their friends and even go to school. Maybe it was Frankie's parents who cut her off from the outside world. I don't know. A couple of times I went up to the house and posted letters through the box at the gate. I got no reply but I continued to send messages until just before we went off for our summer holiday.

By now the streets of Dartmouth were heaving with unknown tourist faces and the river was full of boats. But thoughts of Frankie were never far away. One day I was on the waterfront when a tall ship went by. Music was blasting from its speakers and it was packed with children hanging off the rigging. Some of them were up there in wheelchairs, would you believe. Everybody was waving to them, and they were waving back, happy and excited. They didn't know what lay ahead of them, out there on the waiting sea, but they had everything to hope for – a whole summer of adventure – and life felt good.

I watched them disappearing down the river and heard their music fading. 'Always Look on the Bright Side' – that's what they were playing. It made me think of Frankie, so full of hope as well. Now I only have to hear that music and I see her in her father's car, driving away, me waving after her, knowing that she couldn't even wave back.

The Cancer Expert

Back home again I found Mum in the attic digging out tents and sleeping bags for the camping holiday in Scotland that she, Dad and I were setting off on next day. Normally she'd be in high old spirits about leaving our little cramped house behind and going off for a couple of weeks. But this time she was leaving Damo, and I put her quietness down to worrying about what he'd get up to on his own, and what state the house would be in when we returned.

We packed the car together in near silence. A couple of times I tried to reassure Mum by saying things about Damo being perfectly capable of looking after himself, and Grandma making sure that there were no wild parties. Finally, however, she admitted that it wasn't Damo she was worrying about – it was some friend of hers from the hospital where she worked these days as a secretary.

As Mum rarely ever went so far as to describe

anybody as a friend, I can remember feeling surprised. But not surprised enough to ask any questions, and Mum didn't have the time to talk anyway – she was too busy getting us packed up.

Early next morning we set off. Dad had an arrangement with a cousin in Shropshire who'd agreed to swap his camper van for our car. We drove up there, stayed the night, had a bit of family time, then carried on next day, heading for Loch Lomond, where we were booked into a campsite for the first couple of nights before moving on up to the Highlands.

The weather was good and the forecast even better. It was great to be on the road, with no cares in the world. The loch was beautiful and, as we pulled into the campsite, I felt a world away from Dartmouth.

At least I did until Mum produced a brand-new mobile phone and started calling this friend of hers from the hospital. As she never phoned anybody, always saying she hated mobiles, I was taken aback, and I think Dad was as well.

'How's it going? . . . Thinking of you . . . Phone any time you want to talk . . . You know that, don't you? . . . Feel so guilty leaving you.'

After that, every day was the same. Mum texted every morning and was on the phone every night.

She never explained who she was talking to, or why, and I remember thinking how crazy she was for bringing her troubles on holiday with her. Holidays were for leaving things like that behind.

That's how I was about Frankie.

I scarcely can admit it now, because I'm so ashamed. But, to begin with on that holiday, the relief of getting away from Frankie was overwhelming. I hadn't realised how much I'd been worrying about her. But now, just by being out of Dartmouth, I felt set free. It was wonderful not to be thinking about cancer all the time. Wonderful to put Frankie behind me and think about other things.

But then one evening I was pulled up short. We were heading up the west coast, aiming to do a bit of island-hopping. It was late and we'd only just arrived at our campsite, having failed to calculate how long our journey would take. We hadn't eaten yet. It was dark and we hadn't even set up our camp, but yet again Mum was on the phone.

'How's it going?' I heard her say as I started digging down the food bag, wondering what we were going to eat. 'How are you coping? And Frankie, how's she?'

Frankie!

When Mum came off the phone, I wanted to know everything. That was when I found out about

Mum knowing Mrs Bradley from their choir days. Incredibly, she was the friend Mum had been phoning. A while ago now, they'd bumped into each other at the hospital when Mrs Bradley had been trying to figure out the best treatment for her daughter. Mum had shown her round and a burgeoning friendship had been set in motion.

'Mrs Bradley was very impressed with the Royal South Hams,' Mum said. 'But then, she would be. Their facilities speak for themselves. They're obviously world-class. And Eustace Herbert's world-class too. I don't care what some people say about treatment in America – Frankie Bradley could do no better than be put in his care. At least that's what I told her mother, and she agreed.'

A chill wind blew through me. 'Mrs Bradley does know that you're only a secretary?' I said, remembering the local cancer expert that Frankie had told me about.

'Of course she does,' Mum answered. 'I'm sure she does. Well, I *think* she does. But what's that got to do with anything? Really, Charis, you do ask the strangest questions. What if she doesn't? The facts are the same, so what difference does it make?'

I didn't answer. But from that moment onwards I knew that my mum had been Mrs Bradley's so-called local cancer expert and that, if Frankie's treatment didn't work, it would be her fault. I felt sick. Felt to blame. I'd been so slow. I should have realised long ago.

After this, I started phoning Frankie and leaving voicemails and texts. Every time Mum got in touch with Mrs Bradley, waves of guilt surged through me and I'd try again. Frankie never replied, but the messages I left got longer and longer. Scotland was beautiful and I was determined that she should share it with me. It was the least I could do.

But the more I wrote, the longer it took and, the longer it took, the less I wanted to write and, the less I wanted to write, the more tedious the messages became. I tried throwing in jokes to spice them up, but my messages were painful stuff.

Finally Frankie texted back, putting me out of my misery. Impatiently, she informed me that I sounded like an electronic tour guide that had been left switched on, and could I stop it, please. Chemotherapy was hell, she said, and my phoney cheerfulness wasn't making it any better. In fact, if I really cared about her, I wouldn't get in touch at all. My silence was the best thing I could do for her. She was fed up with hearing from me.

I felt deeply offended, but ashamed as well, because I knew I'd brought it on myself. For the rest of the holiday, I moped around, wanting to put things right but not knowing how. There had to be something I could do to make it up to Frankie for being such a lousy friend.

It wasn't until the journey home, however, that it came to me. The day was far too hot for travelling, but we had no choice. Picking up our car in Shropshire, we steamed down one motorway after another until the River Severn opened out on one side of us, spanned by the Severn Bridge, and suddenly the sky ahead of us was full of hot-air balloons.

It must have been a convention or something like that. Balloons of every shape and size drifted overhead, carried on invisible breezes. They looked so magical and free, and it was then that I had my idea.

As I watched the balloons floating away across the Severn estuary, something Frankie had once said came back to me. It had been just before her operation. She'd wanted me to fix up for her to go flying, and I'd said I'd look into it but never had. She hadn't mentioned it again and I'd forgotten all about it, happy to let it go because it had been such a big request and I hadn't known where to start.

But now I did. Ballooning, I thought. That was something I could do for Frankie. There must be clubs that I could phone to get her flying, like she always wanted. Make it happen. Give her a surprise. That's what I'd do. I'd make it my treat.

Johnny Depp

We returned home to find Damo, Grandma and Judith Mason enjoying a perfect summer's afternoon in the garden. A table had been carried out and laid with a pretty cloth and sultana scones and jam. Tea was in a china pot instead of Grandma's usual teabags in mugs, and the sugar even came in lumps, in a little bowl with Grandma's best silver tongs.

Mum only had to climb up the steps from the street, laden with sleeping bags and stuff from the car, and her annoyance was plain to see. 'What's going on here, then?' she said, trying to sound casual, although it didn't come across that way.

Judith Mason rose to her feet as if she couldn't help but catch Mum's drift. It was good to see us again, she said, but time was getting on and she really ought to leave.

Dad tried persuading her to stay, but Judith

slipped away, saying that Grandma would be wanting to hear all our holiday news. 'She's been missing you,' she said.

'It looks like it,' Mum said.

Everybody laughed awkwardly, except for Judith Mason, who hurried away. Dad looked embarrassed. Grandma looked put out. It wasn't exactly the best of home-comings. Then, when we got indoors, Mum was astonished to find the whole place clean and tidy. She'd been braced for Damo to have wrecked the joint, but it was dusted and spotless and the oven even contained a casserole that Damo could never have prepared all by himself.

Angrily, Mum demanded an explanation. But she knew, before Damo explained, that Judith Mason had been in her house.

'She was only helping,' Damo said. 'It was meant to be a nice surprise.'

Mum looked at Damo as if he was mad, and he did what he was best at – headed for the door. When he was gone, Dad tried to smooth things over. But it was impossible; Mum was too angry. She felt violated in her own home, she said, throwing out the casserole and refusing to let us eat it. What had that woman been thinking of? No way, *no way ever*, would she stick her nose in someone else's house.

Poor old Mum – she wasn't happy until she'd

emptied our camping gear all over Judith Mason's housework, messing everything up. 'That's better,' she said, adding dirty washing for good measure, and muddy boots.

But it still didn't feel quite like home and next morning, when she and I went up the garden to hang out our holiday washing, it didn't look like it either. In the two weeks we'd been away, our garden had blossomed into someone else's. All sorts of flowers that hadn't been seen for years – roses, lupins, poppies, lavender – had opened out. Even a vegetable garden had sprung into life.

Since Grandad's day, we'd never had a vegetable garden. But now lettuces were coming up, along with cucumbers, tomatoes, climbing beans, cabbages, beetroots and sweetcorn. Mum was stunned to silence when she saw them all and so was I.

But later Mum had plenty to say. It was obvious that Judith Mason was after something, she announced that evening when Dad came in with a basket full of lettuces, handfuls of climbing beans and a huge bunch of roses, especially for her.

'Here we go again,' Dad said, standing in the doorway looking rattled. *'After something?* What's that meant to mean?'

He and Mum didn't row outright, but for the rest of the night they moved round each other in studied silence, having occasional little digs. It was a shame, Dad said, that Mum couldn't recognise an act of kindness when it hit her in the face. And equally it was a shame, Mum retorted, that a fine, upstanding man like Dad could be bought so cheaply with peas and climbing beans.

At the time I thought that she was being unfair. But, in the weeks to come, I saw what she meant. Dad was obviously impressed by Judith Mason. He talked about her all the time, even though he knew Mum didn't like it. And, when she came round with her hoe and wheelbarrow, he was always out there in a flash, offering to help even though he was supposed to hate gardening.

There was a terrible atmosphere in the house. I started to develop a major aversion to Judith Mason for what she was doing. I hated the sight of Dad dancing around like her little lapdog and hated the familiarity with which she greeted me every time we met, acting as if we were old friends. She could have my dad, I told myself, but she couldn't have his family. We weren't to be bought.

'That woman's a cunning piece of work,' Mum announced one day, right out of the blue. 'She's a nest of vipers disguised as a gardener. She might be short and dumpy and have bad hair, but by God does she need watching!'

Damo was around when Mum said that. Against all evidence to the contrary, he laughed at the idea of Judith Mason being interested in a clapped-out bloke like Dad. Why would she want him, he wanted to know, when she'd got a toy boy of her own back at home?

'What do you mean, a toy boy?' Mum and I both said together.

'Don't you know?' Damo said. 'Haven't you heard? Judith Mason's living with a man half her age. Johnny Something, I think he's called. Now, what was it? Oh, I know, *Johnny Depp*.'

I blushed. Damo laughed as if he'd scored a point. Mum came to my defence, telling him to leave his sister alone. 'You have to be talking about John Bepp,' she said. 'Our new young choirmaster. The one who robbed me of my chance to sing. So, he lives with Judith Mason. *Now why doesn't that surprise me?*'

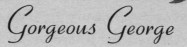

Gorgeous George

The day after hearing about Judith Mason and John Bepp, I received a voicemail from Frankie. In a sheepish voice, she apologised for the angry text message she'd sent me while I was in Scotland and asked if we could still be friends.

I was so relieved to hear from her that I replied straight away, even though I was back at school and halfway through a French class. I apologised for my own string of terrible messages and said that of course we were still friends.

After that, it didn't take much arm twisting on Frankie's part to get me to agree to a bit more boat 'borrowing'. 'I want to see you,' she said. 'I'm missing you, but I can't get out. Not on my own. So come up to the house. Come tonight. I'll stay awake for you.'

Last time I'd gone up to Bradley Castle in the night, the river had been so high and fast that I'd been lucky to get across it. This time, however, the water was as calm as a millpond and I could have swum across to Kingswear if I hadn't found a boat.

I crossed the river easily and started up the hill. I was nervous about seeing Frankie again after all this time. Nervous about how I'd find her and what the chemotherapy might be doing. What I remember most, however, when I reached the house, wasn't the rings round Frankie's eyes or the weight she'd lost.

It was her hair.

Last time I'd seen Frankie, she'd been shaven bald. But now she had hair again that looked so natural that, stupidly and against all logic, I guessed it must have grown back. And, if it had grown, I told myself, that had to be an indication that Frankie was getting better.

We walked round the garden, up and down the terraces, across the tennis court and back up to the house. It was the middle of September, but the night was as warm as July. I remember how happy I was. Suddenly I felt as if I had a future again, just because Frankie had one too. All this time I'd worried that the chemotherapy would zap not only her cancer cells, but the rest of her as well. And yet here she was, her old self, cracking jokes, remembering the past and looking forward to the future.

Only when we went up to Frankie's bedroom did the mood change. It happened the minute she opened her door and I saw all her white rugs gone, and her blue-and-silver decorations. Shelves and surfaces had been wiped clean, curtains had been replaced by blinds and the room smelt like a hospital. There were no personal things lying around any more. The flowers had gone. Even the cards had gone.

I didn't understand, and Frankie explained that her parents had done this because of the risk of infection caused by her immune system being weakened by chemotherapy. According to the hospital, standards of hygiene needed to be of the highest order.

'What they meant was avoiding people with sore throats,' Frankie said, 'and public places like swimming pools. I don't think gutting my bedroom ever crossed their minds. But then, that's Mummy and Daddy for you.'

I stood on the threshold, scarcely daring to go in for fear of polluting all those pristine surfaces with germs. Frankie dragged me in, then went to the dressing table – and removed her hair. It came off in one piece, which she hung on the mirror. Underneath it she was still bald, and it was as much as I could do not to shriek.

'Your hair's a wig,' I gasped.

'Of course it is,' Frankie replied. 'What else did you think?'

'I thought it was your real hair,' I said.

Frankie laughed. 'It *is* my real hair,' she said. 'Mummy saved it in a bag when I went to the hairdresser's, then took it to some big-deal wig maker who works for ballet and opera companies and had it made up. It cost a fortune, which is why it looks so convincing.'

She was delighted to have fooled me. I went and took a closer look, and even then it still looked real. She cracked a joke at my expense, and I tried to crack one back but found myself awkward and tongue-tied.

Suddenly the future I'd seen for both of us had been snatched away. I looked at Frankie. Looked at the rings round her eyes and the weight she'd lost. Far from being cured, as I'd wanted to believe, she was still quite obviously ill. And far from being her old self, there was something restless about her – something sharp and scratchy, despite the jokes. Something *different* that I hadn't noticed until now.

'How much longer will your treatment last?' I said.

'I don't know,' Frankie replied. 'But I'm doing very well, apparently. In fact, Dr Herbert says I'm doing brilliantly.'

Dr Herbert was every bit as gorgeous as Frankie had first thought, though with one fatal flaw – he was married. She produced a photograph of him and requested that I hang it in the throne room in place of Orlando Bloom. I said it must be serious if she wanted me to do that.

'Love's a funny thing,' Frankie cooed.

I said it was indeed, and told her about Dad making a fool of himself with our gardening lady. Then Frankie told me about a stable girl her dad had done the same with.

'Perhaps what's happened is that your dad's fallen in love with gardening,' she said. 'That's what my dad said. It wasn't the girl, he said. It was the horses. But Mum got rid of the girl anyway.'

By this time, I was beginning to think I ought to be leaving. Before I said anything, however, Frankie asked if I'd like to look through her clothes. Because she'd lost so much weight, nothing fitted any more.

'Mummy says that when I'm better we're going on a shopping trip together,' she said, crossing to her wardrobe and sliding back the doors. 'All of these are going, so you can take what you like.'

More clothes than I'd ever seen in one place at the same time hung before me. Frankie started pulling things out. None of them was right for me because our shapes and tastes were different, but I ended up trying things on anyway, and surprised myself with how good some of them looked. For a while that night, the two of us forgot Frankie's chemotherapy treatment and anything to do with illnesses as we zipped, buttoned and struggled into and out of clothes, covering the floor with them, throwing them about and generally raising enough dust to disable Frankie's immune system for the next ten years.

I was giggling uncontrollably, struggling out of a dress that was way too small, when her brother, Gorgeous George, walked in. I hadn't seen him close up since that day in Green Flax, and squawked and pulled the dress around me to hide my naked bits. At least he had the decency to look away. When he looked again, I was back in my own clothes, my face bright red.

'What's going on here?' he said, sounding more like Frankie's father than a nineteen-year-old brother who was just about to go off to university.

'What does it look like?' Frankie replied. 'We're trying on clothes.'

'At four in the morning?' George said.

'What's wrong with that?' Frankie said.

'What's wrong is that you look exhausted,' George said. Then, turning to me, 'And who are *you*?

I've seen you before, I'm sure I have.'

No way was I owning up to being the girl in Green Flax. Not that I got a chance, because Gorgeous George escorted me off the property. Some girls would have given their eye teeth to be escorted by George Bradley, but it wasn't like that, believe me. He marched me down the hill, helped me find where I'd left the boat, stuck me in it and saw me off, saying that he wouldn't tell his parents this time but heaven help me if it happened again.

'My sister's very, very sick,' he said, 'in case you hadn't noticed, and you've just jeopardised her life, coming round here with your germs. So, if you're any sort of friend, you'll keep away until her treatment's over. And if you can't do that, I'll find a way to help you. Have you got that? *Good!*'

Next day, Frankie phoned to apologise for George. He could be a pain sometimes, she said, but he wasn't always like that, honestly. It was just that he was worried on her behalf, and so was Diggers. These days they were more like a pair of little old extra parents than teenage boys. She shouldn't eat this, she shouldn't do that, she'd got to rest, she'd got to keep on fighting and thinking positive thoughts.

'It's driving me crazy,' Frankie said. 'They're always on at me about something. If the cancer doesn't finish me off, there's a strong possibility that my family will. All I want is to be my old self again, but in their eyes I'm just a poor sick girl.'

I said that, when I thought of Frankie, the words 'poor' and 'sick' never came to mind, but 'life' did instead. Frankie liked that. She said she wished her family could see things that way, and that the inhabitants of Kingswear and Dartmouth could too. Apparently it wasn't just her family who were acting weird these days. It was the entire neighbourhood.

'I know I should be grateful for all this sympathy,' Frankie confessed, 'but having strangers out there pitying me makes my skin crawl. I feel like a soap opera, with the world outside my window full of viewers. I'll give you an example of what it's like. There's this one woman who Mummy hardly knows, and she texts every morning and phones every night. Just because she's a cancer expert and once gave Mum a bit of advice, she seems to think that gives her the right. She hardly knows us, but she acts like family. As if we don't have enough to put up with – and now we've got some nutter stalking us!'

A Round of Applause

I knew who the stalker was, of course, because I'd heard Mum make the calls. And, much to my surprise, I took offence. Never in a million years would I have imagined siding with Mum against my friend, but that's what I did, because Frankie's words hurt.

Suddenly I felt insulted on Mum's behalf. If I'd been ill, I told myself, and half of Dartmouth had been phoning to ask how I was, I'd have been touched. But Frankie had this princess side that took people for granted. She was a Bradley and she thought things were her due.

What I should have done was explain to Frankie how I felt, and get the whole thing off my chest. But I'm a bottler, not a blower – I'm the sort who stores things up. So, when Frankie called my mum a stalker, I didn't protest. Instead I paid her back by doing what her mum was doing to mine and ignoring her calls.

It was petty and I knew it. After all, poor Frankie had no idea that she'd insulted my mum. After a couple of weeks of silence, she started bombarding me with voicemail messages and texts, wanting to know what was up. Was something wrong at home? Had my dad run off with the gardening lady? Did I want to talk?

In the end, feeling guilty, I came clean. 'That woman you were telling me about,' I explained on the phone. 'The one who rings and texts your mother all the time . . .'

'What about her?' Frankie said.

'She's my mum.'

Frankie laughed. She saw the funny side straight away. 'You mean the one I called a stalker?' she said.

'I mean the one your mother thinks is a cancer expert,' I replied. 'You know – the one who told her that Dr Herbert was the best cancer specialist in the world.'

'But I thought your mother was a secretary,' Frankie said.

'My mother's Dr Herbert's secretary,' I said.

Frankie laughed at that as well. I said that she had every right to be angry with my mother, because she'd probably ruined her opportunities of better treatment abroad, but that didn't give her the right to call her a stalker and a nutter. Frankie agreed and said that she was sorry. The one thing she didn't agree with, though, was that Mum had ruined her opportunities. In fact, she said, Mum had done her a massive favour because, instead of being jetted off to America, she'd been able to commute into hospital daily and sleep nights in her own bed.

'So instead of accusing your mum of stalking me, I should be thanking her,' Frankie said. 'And I will. I promise you. I'll make it up to her, I swear I will. In fact, I'll make it up to both of you.'

Nothing more was said, but a couple of weeks later an invitation arrived to a lunchtime party that Frankie's mother was holding in aid of cancer research. Accompanying it was a handwritten note from Mrs Bradley, saying that the party marked the end of the chemotherapy sessions and Frankie's getting back her old life, and was therefore the occasion of great celebration.

'Please come,' she wrote. 'And bring your daughter. Francesca says she'd like to meet her.'

On the day in question, Mum and I arrived at Bradley Castle to find ourselves in company with all the great and good of Dartmouth and Kingswear. It was one of those cringe-worthy occasions when you drift around, not knowing what to do or say. Frankie was in the middle of a group of her flamingo friends and couldn't get away, and Mrs

Bradley was always busy with somebody else.

For most of the time, Mum and I made the most of the world-class view and hung around trying to think of things to say to each other. It was a golden occasion – one of those freak October days that could be summer. We ate salmon from the Dartmouth Smokehouse, Mum drank more champagne than she should have done, and I enjoyed sneaking a few glasses myself whenever her back was turned. On one occasion we got into a conversation with some ladies from the choir, who said that Mum was missed. On another occasion the Johncoxes came over and said what a wonderful nanny Grandma had been in her heyday when they'd lived up at the big house on the outskirts of Dartmouth.

But apart from that we were on our own. Waiters glided about, making sure that people's glasses were always full. A little band played on the top terrace and its music drifted down towards us. A couple of times I caught Frankie looking our way, as if she wanted to come over. Once she nearly made it, but was nabbed by her mother before she could.

Mrs Bradley was quite plainly the queen of the occasion. Delight that her daughter's treatment was over radiated out of her. In fact, she absolutely glowed. After everybody had eaten, she conducted an auction in aid of cancer research, raising a sum that had everybody gasping when it was announced. You could see how proud she was. She made a speech about thinking positive, which she said was the key to Frankie's recovery, along with carrot juice and the Royal South Hams, whose Dr Herbert was the best cancer specialist in the world.

Over on the far side of the terrace, Frankie winked at me, and I winked back. She was trying to look as if she was enjoying herself, but I could see how tired she was. She was seated on a swing seat, surrounded by presents that people had bought for her. I felt sorry for her. This party was meant to be celebrating getting back her life, but this wasn't the life she wanted. This was Frankie's mother's life, not hers. It might have been hers once, but not any more. Being ill had changed her.

Finally shadows started creeping across the garden and the party drew to a close. People started drifting towards their cars and I looked around for Frankie, wanting to say goodbye. At first I couldn't find her, but then I caught sight of her without her wig, scratching her head.

If Frankie had taken off all her clothes, people couldn't have been more embarrassed. All around her they were looking away. Frankie glanced at me, bald-headed and triumphant. *This is the real me*, the glance seemed to say. *Not some perfect Frankie, living some perfect life. But the person I really am, living my real life.*

And I applauded her for it. I mean that, literally, physically. I put my two hands together and gave her a clap. In the awkward silence something had to be done – and I was the one who did it.

For a moment everybody was aghast, but then, to my astonishment, Diggers Bradley put his hands together, as if he too understood what Frankie was trying to say, and then goodness only knows why but the Johncoxes did it as well, and soon everybody was applauding, including Mrs Bradley – although she didn't look very pleased about it.

When I got home, there was hell to pay. Mum kept her mouth shut all the way to Clarence Street. Then, as soon as the door was closed behind us, she started on about what an embarrassment I'd been. How could I have done that, she wanted to know – drawing attention to Frankie in such an obvious fashion, and drawing attention to myself? Couldn't I see how much embarrassment I was causing? Poor, poor Frankie! And her mother – she'd looked as if she'd wanted to die.

Next morning, Mum bought chocolates for Frankie and flowers for her mother, and tried to make me take them up and apologise. But my friendship with Frankie wasn't Mum's to organise. It was private, thank you very much. I agreed to give the flowers to Mrs Bradley, partly to keep Mum happy and partly because I felt sorry for the embarrassment I'd caused. But I point blank refused to give Frankie the chocolates.

Not that I got the chance anyway. When I arrived at Bradley Castle, Mrs Bradley kept me at the gate and would only speak on the intercom. She accepted my apology, saying that the 'little incident' had been forgotten, and told me to leave the flowers at the gate. But I knew it wasn't really forgotten and wouldn't be for a long time either. I'd meant to honour Frankie when I'd put my hands together. But, in her mother's eyes, I'd brought shame on her head.

Book Three

Gold Doubloons

The day of the party might have felt like summer but within a week the trees had been stripped bare, the roads were full of dead leaves and a cold wind had come blowing in off the sea, bringing weather almost bleak enough for January. Autumn had caught up with us at last – savage, brief and tipping us straight into winter.

Often the winters are warm in Dartmouth compared to other places around the country, but not that year. I managed one final visit to Castle Cove, where I took down a photograh of Dr Herbert and hung it, pride of place. But, with the wind whipping up the beach, I wondered how long it would last.

Dartmouth can seem like an entirely different place on a wild winter's day. Even the river's a different shape – faster and bigger and all rucked up. On a summer's day, it can make the town seem almost exotic. But if the winter is stormy, Dartmouth feels like a Wild West town. The sea is like a prairie wilderness at its door, vast and unpeopled, and the streets are unpeopled too. Everybody's shut up at home (either that or in the pub) and the only gossip you ever hear is months old, because there's never anything new to talk about.

But there was always one good thing about winter, and that was our birthdays. Frankie's came before mine, in the middle of November and, as it approached that year, I remembered the promise I'd made about flying. Still I'd done nothing about it, for all my good intentions. Frankie hadn't mentioned it since, but that was no excuse. I had promised, and now here was her birthday, coming up fast, and I decided it was time to put things right.

So I got on the Internet and found a ballooning company somewhere near Bristol that was desperately expensive but cheaper than all the rest. I bought a flight voucher for Frankie, putting down a small deposit. But, given that this was meant to be a present, how was I going to pay for the rest?

I didn't have a clue. Certainly earning money by doing jobs round the house would never raise the money fast enough. And I knew no one would lend it to me, not even Damo.

I tried him, though, just to see.

'I don't know why you've come to me,' he said.

'Because you've got a job and I haven't,' I pleaded. 'And there's nothing else here in Dartmouth to spend your money on other than drink and drugs.'

Damo looked at me as if he was shocked. 'What are you saying? I don't do drugs,' he said.

'I'm not saying you do,' I replied. 'But I know what half your friends do. I'm not an idiot. It's local knowledge. And you've got to admit that lending me money has to be more worthwhile than that.'

Damo agreed. I was right, he said, but if he had any spare money he wouldn't be spending it on drugs – he'd be spending it on a flat instead of living at home with us.

'Besides, what do you want the money for?' he said.

This was the question I couldn't answer. If anyone in our family knew how much money I was planning to spend on a girl like Frankie, who was rolling in it anywhere, they'd have had a fit.

'Forget it,' I said. 'Sorry I asked.'

Damo was curious, but could get no more out of me. No way was I telling him anything that could end up being common knowledge down at the Dolphin. Instead, in desperation because Frankie's birthday was drawing closer, I turned my attention to the most unlikely option available – the secret hoard of money that Dad was supposed to have hidden under the pigpen.

For years there had been this rumour circulating that my skinflint dad had a treasure hoarded up (under the pigpen, of all places), possibly in gold doubloons. According to Damo – who was the one I blamed for this whole ridiculous thing – at one time there'd actually been talk down in the Dolphin of getting up a digging party.

When I'd heard that, I remember pleading with Dad to make a public announcement that there was no money. The thought of people crawling round our garden in the dark was more than I could bear.

But Dad had laughed at my discomfort, tapping the side of his nose and saying, 'But what if it's true? What if I *do* have a garden full of gold doubloons?'

Dad had been teasing me, of course. Or at least I'd told myself he had. But now, with nothing else to hope for, my mind turned to digging up the garden myself. It was a long shot, I knew. More than a long shot, it was downright ridiculous. I, more than anyone, knew that Dad's secret gold was a myth. But digging for treasure was better than phoning Frankie to ask if she minded paying for her own birthday treat!

At any rate, that's what I told myself.

So, every day after school, I sneaked up the garden to dig as much as I could before Mum and Dad came home from work. It was a nasty business, digging in the semi-darkness for gold that I was 99.9 per cent sure didn't exist. The pigpen was full of logs that Dad had stored for the winter, and they all had to be moved before I could start, and put back afterwards in exactly the right place so that no one would know I'd been there.

'Why am I doing this?' I kept asking myself, covered in mud, never knowing what nasty thing I'd put my hand on next. And there never was an answer. Leastways, not one that made any sense.

Then, one afternoon, Damo found me at it. I pretended to be getting into gardening, just like Dad, but he didn't believe me.

'What are you really up to?' he said.

'I'm not up to anything,' I replied.

'Tell that to the fairies,' Damo said.

'I mean it,' I said.

'You wouldn't by any chance be digging for gold?' he said.

'Of course not,' I replied.

'I'm glad to hear it,' he said. 'Because I wouldn't want you to be wasting your time.'

He went away laughing to himself, leaving me feeling like a fool, because he was right – I *was* wasting my time. And yet, within days of that, I'd struck lucky.

It was a Saturday morning and I had the whole place to myself because Mum and Dad had taken the car to be repaired, Damo was still asleep and Grandma must have been as well, since her curtains were still drawn. With no one around to question what I was doing, I sneaked up the garden to tackle the final corner of the pigpen. This required moving a pile of flowerpots stacked up right at the back and, as soon as I lifted the first of them, I dislodged the rest – with the result that gold coins started rolling everywhere.

Dad *did* have treasure after all. And he hadn't even bothered to bury it. I got down on my hands and knees, unable to believe what lay before me. Soon there must have been about thirty coins, large and small, gathered in my lap. They weren't as heavy as I'd imagine a treasure trove of gold doubloons would be. But age definitely hadn't dimmed their lustre.

I examined them closely, one by one. Words were written on them in a language I couldn't read. But gold has its own language and there was no mistaking their beauty.

In the end, I took a couple of them (which I reckoned would be enough) and stacked the rest back in the flowerpots. I didn't stop to think that this might count as stealing. I was too indignant. All these years of scrimping and going without, and Dad had had this treasure hidden up the garden all along! What other secrets had he hidden? I asked myself. In fact, who was he? Did I really know my father? Where had all these gold doubloons come from? How had he got hold of them?

Unable to answer any of these questions, but determined to make the most of my windfall, I decided to go down to the bank to change my two coins into proper money. In my strange state of suspended disbelief, it seemed the obvious thing to do, no more complicated than changing pounds into euros. The only problem I foresaw was that news of Dad's pirate hoard might get out.

I wasn't aware of knowing anybody who worked in the bank but, just to be on the safe side, I disguised myself with one of Mum's headscarves and Damo's sunglasses. When my turn came at the counter, I thrust the gold coins under the grille with my hands cupped over them so that no one else would see.

'I don't know how much these are worth,' I whispered, afraid of setting off a Klondike gold rush in the queue behind me, 'but I'd like them changed into pounds.'

The bank lady stared down at my coins. For someone who was in the presence of what was probably pirate treasure plundered from the Spanish Main, she looked distinctly unimpressed.

'And exactly how many pounds are you hoping I'll give you for these?' she said, her voice wobbling somewhere between amusement and irritation.

'I don't know,' I said. 'You're the bank person. You tell me. But notes would be preferable, otherwise I won't be able to carry it all.'

The bank lady thrust the coins back under the grille. 'Nice try,' she whispered. 'Ha ha. Very funny.' Then, in a louder voice, 'Next customer please.'

I flushed angrily. I didn't understand. I was a valid customer who'd queued for my moment at the counter just like everybody else. I pushed the coins back, demanding to know what was the bank lady's problem.

'My problem,' she said, not bothering to whisper any more, 'is that a queue of people is right behind you, all waiting for their turn. They're people with real business to attend to and you're holding them up. So, please take your toy-town treasure trove and move along.'

When I got home, I found Damo laughing. He pretended he wasn't, but I knew laughter when I heard it – and I knew what it was about. All the way to the bank, I'd believed I had gold in my pocket, but all the way home I'd known otherwise. Of course it wasn't gold! It mightn't be as soft as the chocolate coins you get in Christmas stockings, but it wasn't far off. When I'd bitten one of those coins, it had dented and a bit of tin had fallen off, revealing plastic underneath.

Even now, I still blush at the fool I made of myself that day. Even when I bit into that coin, I was still trying to hang onto my dream. But once I saw Damo's laughing face and went into my bedroom and found a brand-new Captain Jack Sparrow's Pirate Quiz board game sitting on my bed, its money chest empty as if to say *ha*, *ha*, I could no longer deny it – I'd been had.

Hard Times

I told Frankie what had happened, and it came out about the balloon flight. I expected her to be touched and grateful, maybe even to say nice things about what a great friend I was, but her only comment was that ballooning was for wimps. It wasn't risky enough. If she was going flying, she said, she'd want it to be something exciting like hang-gliding or sky-diving, not sitting in some boring wicker basket floating about.

'Not that I do want to go flying,' she added. 'I might have once, but I don't any more. These days just keeping going is hard enough.'

Feeling something between relief and disappointment, I phoned the balloon company and tried to get my deposit back on the flight voucher. I certainly didn't argue with Frankie. If she said that life was hard, I reckoned she must know what she was talking about.

Apart from anything else, she was back at school now and struggling to catch up. She had lessons coming out of her ears, she said, including extra tuition every night at home. Hardly surprisingly, she didn't phone much around that time and, when she did, she always sounded tired and irritable. Everything was too much effort. It wasn't just flying, it was the whole of life. Even finding the time to text or email was difficult. And meeting for even a quick milkshake in Alf Resco's was impossible.

How could we keep a friendship going in an atmosphere like that? Once Frankie and I met up on the street and stood talking in a shop doorway, but neither of us could relax. Frankie kept glancing at her watch because she was meant to be meeting her mother at the gym. Not that she wanted to attend a gym, she said, but she had no choice in the matter.

'Ever since my treatment finished, my family's gone fitness crazy,' Frankie said. 'They've always been fairly sporty anyway, but now they're off the scale. Cars are banned and everybody's got to walk everywhere. My father jogs down to the newsagent's every morning instead of having his paper delivered, and he's given up his cigars. Mummy spends all her time baking organic, stone-ground bread and making us eat fruit and cancer-busting vegetables like carrots. Ugh, carrots!'

She pulled a face. I made sympathetic noises. Frankie said her mother's mantra of thinking positive now ruled their lives. She even attended meetings on the subject, telling people that she knew what she was talking about because look at her daughter, who was cured from cancer, proving that the right mental attitude – and the right food – counted for more than any chemotherapy.

'So I'm a role model,' Frankie said. 'Can you imagine anything worse?'

We walked round to the gym together. Frankie looked tired to me, not like anybody's picture of a role model. But she said that her mother had even written a book, aiming to raise money for cancer research.

'It's gone off to a string of publishers,' she said, 'and Mummy's waiting to see if any of them will take it. It's full of all her favourite cancer-busting recipes, as tested out on me.'

She pulled a face again. Her illness had become an industry, she said. It had given her mother a whole new career.

We parted round the corner from the gym, in case her mother should see us together. For the other problem we faced was that, ever since the day of the lunch party, her mother had taken against me. I only had to be on the phone and Mrs Bradley would be there, trying to get Frankie away. And the situation wasn't helped by Mum taking offence because Mrs Bradley no longer answered her calls.

'The rich are different from the rest of us,' she said. 'I read that somewhere and it's true. They're all over you when they want something, but, once they've got it, you're dropped.'

As we parted, Frankie apologised for grumbling so much. 'I'm sorry,' she said. 'I know it's a pain, but there's nothing I can do.'

I said that friendship was more than just milk-shakes at Alf Resco's – it was something that happened inside. Frankie liked that. She said I had a way with words.

No matter what words I used, however, we didn't see each other again for ages. Both our birthdays passed and we didn't even get to speak. On mine, Mum dragged me off to a concert by her old choir. I don't know why she did that. Maybe she had cheap tickets or something. But it certainly wasn't the sort of thing I was likely to enjoy, and Mum came out downright miserable, saying it was amazing what bad taste people had.

As we were walking away, John Bepp came rushing up to greet us. He said that no one had Mum's lovely, pure, sweet voice, and why didn't she come back? He sounded to me like he meant it, but Mum took the view that he was rubbing salt into her wounds and she stomped off into the night.

'That John Bepp can take his offer and throw it in the Dart,' she said as we steamed up Clarence Street. 'No way would I sing in his choir again.'

It wasn't quite the birthday I'd have organised for myself. And, to compound my misery, it coincided with a party two doors down, organised by Bryony Rogers because her mother was away and her sister was left in charge. Bryony was always having people round and making a noise, but this time it seemed she'd invited half of Dartmouth. Even inside our house with the doors and windows shut, you could still hear music and laughter booming from down the road.

What an ending to my birthday! I went to bed, feeling sorry for myself. It was all very well going on about friendship being something that happened inside. But if I never saw my only friend, what was the point in having one?

I lay awake for ages, looking for someone to blame – and it didn't take long. If I was without a friend to share my birthday with, it was all our mothers' fault – Mrs Bradley's for keeping Frankie away and Mum's for, well, just being Mum. Why was she so prickly? Why had she got to take offence? Why couldn't she make friends like other people

did, and get it right, and not either be all over people, phoning all the time, or not speaking to them?

What Mum needed to do was lighten up, I
thought. It was what they both needed, her and Mrs
Bradley too. But I didn't know how to make it happen. What I did know, though, was that unless I
thought of something, my friendship with Frankie
was doomed.

The DSMCE

It didn't take long to come up with a plan. In fact, the germs of it came that very night, with Bryony Rogers's party banging through the wall. To begin with it was fairly rough around the edges, but I was convinced that, in essence, it had the power to mend fences and bring our two mothers together.

The key to everything, I reckoned, was getting our mothers to laugh. Friendship, it seemed to me from experience, was built around humour more than anything else. If we could get our mothers sharing a joke together, then anything was possible. And I had a cunning idea how to bring it about.

I hugged myself in the darkness, imagining the laughter that my idea might generate after the initial embarrassment had died down. It was a great idea, I told myself. Brilliant, though I said so myself. That it might have the opposite effect to the one desired, driving our mothers even further apart, never crossed my mind.

But then, to be fair, when I put it to Frankie next day, it didn't cross her mind either. She texted straight back, much to my surprise, agreeing that the idea was brilliant.

The whole thing was built around our mothers being open to flattery and having secret desires. Desire – as I had discovered when Damo filled the pigpen with plastic gold – was capable of blinding people to the truth. And so was flattery. That was why wizened old billionaires ended up marrying girls who said they loved them for themselves. And, according to Mum, it was why Dad spent half his time following Judith Mason round like a pet dog.

That day I composed two letters, one to each of our mothers, and emailed them to Frankie to see what she thought. Her reply came back that night, just as I was falling asleep.

'Great. Fantastic. Go for it,' she texted.

'Are you sure?' I texted back.

'I've already told you once – I think the idea's brilliant. Every time I think about it, I can't stop laughing,' Frankie replied.

So, like she said, I went for it. Or, to be correct, we both did. Frankie was the one who got hold of the posh-looking writing paper with the watermark and copied onto it a letterhead that she'd nicked from among her father's business papers. And I was the one who put the finishing touches to the letters and then emailed them to her to print out and forge a couple of flashy signatures with her father's gold-nibbed pen. As a nice little finishing touch, she bribed one of her flamingo friends, whose sister lives in London, to get them posted to our mothers from Westminster, so that they'd arrive with a post-mark that wouldn't cause suspicion.

The day after they'd gone out, we were both to be found within range of our respective letter boxes, waiting to see what would happen next.

'Anything at your end?' Frankie kept texting.

'Not yet. How about you?' I kept texting back.

When the post finally arrived, neither of us dared rush to pick it up, for fear of drawing atten-tion to ourselves. It was Saturday morning and everybody was at home in both our families. I don't know about Frankie but, by the time that Dad picked up an envelope with a No. 10 Downing Street crest on it, I was feeling thor-oughly sick. He handed it to Mum, commenting that he couldn't imagine what the Prime Minister wanted to write to her about, and my stomach churned with anticipation.

'What do you mean?' Mum said.

'Well, look. See for yourself,' Dad said.

Mum ripped open the envelope. She'd been on her way out shopping, but sat down instead – and it's a good job she did. Underneath the Downing Street crest this is what her letter said:

Dear Mrs Watts,

For services to choral music in the Devon/Cornwall region, Her Majesty's Government takes great pleasure in informing you that the Distinguished Service Medal for Civil Enterprise (DSMCE) has been awarded.

The presentation ceremony will take place in Exeter Cathedral and be attended by His Royal Highness the Prince of Wales. Further details are provided on the attached document, which we would be grateful if you could return within seven working dasy of receipt of this letter.

Finally, may I take this opportunity of extending to you hearty congratulations on behalf of us all at No. 10.

Yours sincerely

Prime Minister

Mum didn't quite die of shock, but she wasn't far off. She read the letter twice and then, horror of horrors, tears started rolling down her cheeks. She tried to read the letter out loud to us, but her voice was shaking so much that she had to stop.

Dad took it from her and finished it off. Until now I'd been convinced that neither of them would be taken in. But they never had a moment's doubt.

'It just goes to show,' Mum said. 'What you do in life does make a difference. It does get noticed. Sometimes the little people *do* get recognised for what they contribute. There *is* such a thing as justice after all.'

I felt ashamed when she said that. What had I done?

'The Prime Minister,' Mum kept saying, wonder in her voice. 'The Prince of Wales. The DSMCE. This is incredible!'

Dad said he'd never heard of the DSMCE (hardly surprising, since I'd made it up), but Mum said that only showed how ignorant he was. Apparently Frankie's mother said exactly the same thing, according to Frankie when we spoke later. Her father too reckoned he'd never heard of the DSMCE, but her mother said where'd he been all these years? *Everyone* had heard of it.

Her letter (which she read out loud to her family and, later on the phone, to almost everyone she knew) went like this:

Dear Mrs Bradley

For services to cancer research, including the seminal work, *COOKING POSITIVE: A Guide to Beating Cancer by Healthy Eating*, which has been submitted by your publishers, Faber & Faber, Her Majesty's Government takes great pleasure in informing you that the Distinguished Service Medal for Civil Enterprise (DSMCE) has been awarded.

The presentation ceremony will take place in Exeter Cathedral and be attended by His Royal Highness the Prince of Wales. Details are provided on the attached document, which we would be grateful if you could return within seven working days of receipt of this letter.

Finally, may I take this opportunity of extending to you hearty congratulations on behalf of all of us at No. 10.

Yours sincerely

Prime Minister

Frankie said that, after her mother read the letter, she had to pour herself a stiff drink, and then another one after that. 'Your publishers,' she kept on saying. *'Your publishers . . .'* It was two shocks in one, because she hadn't heard from any of the publishers she'd sent her manuscript to, and had almost given up thinking she would.

That she believed the letter was extraordinary. But she did – they both did, and so did all our friends and family. Nobody said that they smelt a rat. A couple of people admitted to never having heard of the DSMCE, but there were twice as many who reckoned they had.

'I can't believe it,' Frankie said every time she texted me. 'We pulled it off. Or, at least, *you* did. You're brilliant. Never in a million years would I have thought up something like this.'

I remember how proud I felt. When Mum went out spending a fortune on clothes to keep up with the dress code outlined in the attachment to her letter, I forced myself to let her go and to not feel guilty. Mum was spending serious money and Dad was allowing it without a murmur of dissent. And it was all because of me.

The sense of power that I experienced was extraordinary. Dad was going to be furious when the truth came out, and so was Mum. But for a while back there I didn't care. The whole thing would be worth it, I told myself, when she and Mrs Bradley came together in Exeter Cathedral and realised what we'd done.

Only the night before did I begin to get cold feet.

'You do know that they're going through with this?' I said to Frankie on the phone, imagining our mothers presenting themselves at what the attachment to their letters described as the 'Designated

Reception Area', expecting to be met by all the other recipients of the DSMCE.

'I know they're going through with it,' Frankie said. 'There was a dodgy moment the other day when Mum nearly phoned her publishers to thank them for recommending her. And then she nearly phoned 10 Downing Street, asking if Dad could come too. But I distracted her. I can't remember how exactly, but it certainly worked. And now she's all ready to go.'

'You think we should let them do it, then?' I said. 'You don't think we should stop them?'

'Are you kidding me?' Frankie retorted. 'This is what we've worked for. This moment when our mothers face each other in their fancy outfits and realise they've been had.'

I shivered. 'But what if they don't think it's funny?' I said.

'They're not going to think it's funny,' Frankie said. 'Not straight away. But they're bound to realise that it was us and, after the initial embarrassment, they'll have to admit we've been pretty clever. And it's then that they'll laugh. They won't be able to help themselves. They'll say, *That's girls for you*, and maybe even plot together to get us back. And why not? We deserve it. But at least they'll be friends by then, and they'll know that we're friends too.'

I allowed myself to be reassured. But by next

morning, setting off for school leaving Mum half-dressed and in a panic, I was doing some serious stressing. What if things didn't go to plan – if the two of them got their times mixed up and never met, or if they did meet and, in their fury at what we'd done, never quite calmed down?

All day in school, I was in a state of nervous agitation. What was happening? Had our mothers arrived yet? Had they found each other? Dared I ever go back home?

By the end of the day, I was good for nothing except hanging around the shops until they closed, texting Frankie but getting no reply. Finally, knowing I couldn't get out of it any more, I dragged myself up Clarence Street. I realised by now that I'd made a terrible miscalculation. Nobody was going to see the funny side of what I'd done, or laugh it off.

Sure enough, a reception committee was waiting as I came through the door. Mum had been set up and she knew who by. She was furious, and so was Dad, who'd shelled out all that money on a new outfit. But it was what I'd done to Mum that got him more than anything.

'How could you be so cruel?' he burst out, before I'd even had time to come clean. 'I just don't understand it. What's your poor mother ever done to you?'

'It was only meant to be a laugh,' I said.

'I don't see anybody laughing,' Dad said.

He was right. You could almost see the steam coming out of Mum's ears, and not even Damo, with his famous sense of humour, could see the funny side. Dad said that, back in her school days, Mum had been the butt of a series of cruel pranks that had taken her years to recover from.

'At least she had until now,' he said. 'But thanks to you, it's all come back.'

I hung my head. I hadn't known that. 'I only meant it as a bit of fun,' I said.

'Jokes are fun, but this was no joke,' Mum said. 'It was downright wicked. Whose idea was it? Yours or the Bradley girl's?'

I didn't even need to answer that one before the two of us were banned from ever seeing each other again. Definitely and forever, it seemed, we were *not* to be friends. We were evil when we got together. Our silly little plan to give our mothers something to laugh at and somehow bring them together had totally misfired.

My phone was taken off me and I didn't know if I'd ever get it back. Next day in school, I emailed Frankie but got no reply. Then I rang her mobile from a call box on the way home. Then I borrowed Damo's mobile without asking and sent a text, then a voicemail. But still I got no reply.

Dark Against the Night Sky

It's incredible how fast Christmas comes round. One minute it's the end of the summer holidays and you're tipping the sand out of your shoes, and the next it's deepest December, the whole of Dartmouth is lit up with ribbons of fairy lights, the Castle Hotel is wrapped up like a Christmas gift and all the holiday houses are occupied again.

Not that any lights were on in Frankie's house. Ever since the day of the joke, Bradley Castle had stood dark against the night sky. It was as if Frankie and her family had disappeared off the face of the earth.

I worried on a daily basis about what I'd done, where Frankie was and how the two of us were ever going to put things right. What a fool I'd been, allowing my misplaced sense of humour to run away with me. What an idiot!

The end of term was full of distractions, but

none was sufficient to give me peace of mind. Christmas passed in a blur. The highlight was snow on Christmas Eve (which we never get in Devon, because it's too far south), but the low point was Boxing Day, when we went round to Grandma's for sherry and mince pies – only to find that Judith Mason had been invited too.

I never want to go through anything like that again. We always went round to Grandma's side of the house on Boxing Day and nobody ever dressed up because it was only us. But Dad dressed up that year, as if he knew that Judith Mason would be there, and from the way that she was kitted out – in a stupid dress with a velvet skirt and tartan bows – you'd have thought she'd been invited to some county ball.

We walked in, all unsuspecting, and there she was, helping Grandma get out the sherry glasses and heat up the mince pies. You'd have thought she was the hostess and we were her guests. Her face was all made up, she'd done something about her terrible straggly hair and she'd even bought us all presents – which meant that Mum had to apologise because we'd bought none for her.

Mum was furious. You can just imagine. And she was even more furious when Dad produced a present of his own, which he presented to Judith to thank her for her *sterling work in our garden*. He raised a toast to her and Mum almost choked.

Afterwards, she and Dad had a terrible argument. Judith Mason had gone off into the night as if she hadn't noticed anything wrong, Grandma had retired to bed and Damo had headed down to the Dolphin, as if he realised what was coming next. I sat on my own up in my bedroom, thinking that Mum looked a million times as good as Judith Mason, even when she didn't bother dressing up, and wondering what Dad saw in his frumpy middle-aged gardener.

Meanwhile, in the living room beneath me, Mum asked Dad more or less the same question, only more loudly and angrily. They were still arguing when I fell asleep. Dad insisted that Judith attracted him about as much as a cold corner in a haunted house, but Mum refused to believe him.

It was the worst possible ending to Christmas. I even cried. I'd never felt so lonely in my life. I wished I'd got my phone and could contact Frankie and tell her all about it. I imagined her off on one of the Bradley family's winter skiing holidays, surrounded by mountains and gorgeous young men.

It was all right for people like them. Whatever happened – cancer, arguments, even murmurings of divorce – they'd always got something waiting in the wings to cheer them up. I wished that I could change places with Frankie – that just for one day she could be me, living my life and putting up with my family, and I could be her, skiing, snow-boarding or whatever she was doing.

Next day Mum and Dad tried to act normally, as if nothing had happened. Even so, you could have cut the atmosphere with a knife. Damo stayed in bed until lunchtime and then went out and didn't come back, and I sat in front of the telly, though I can't remember what I watched.

It was only late at night, after Mum and Dad had gone to bed, having failed to rouse me, that a programme caught my attention. It was on an extreme sport that I'd never heard of before called halo-jumping. I awoke from my sleep to find some man in an oxygen mask crouched in a military-looking plane with the side open, describing what he was about to do as the ultimate sky-dive experience. Given what I think of flying, I nearly turned him off and went to bed. But there must have been something about him that caught my attention, and looking back, I think it was his fear.

The man was sweating like a pig and, when he explained why, I can't say I blamed him. Apparently he was going to leap out of the plane, which was coasting a staggering six miles above ground. And for five life-long minutes before pulling his parachute cord, he intended to fly.

It was going to be cold up there. It was going to be lonely. If anything went wrong with the man's oxygen mask, he was going to be dead. But then, for five long minutes until he pulled that cord, he was risking certain death anyway. If anything went wrong up there – if the man panicked, or lost consciousness, or even momentarily blanked out – he didn't stand a chance.

But if he survived, the man said, he'd been promised the most beautiful five minutes of his life.

I went and sat right in front of the television screen, watching with fascination as the plane reached its destination and the man made his jump. The sky took hold of him and the plane fell away. And suddenly, against that great, vast sky, the man looked like something else – not a person any more, not a bird, but another sort of creature altogether.

The extraordinary thing was that what I was watching looked entirely natural. If it had been me, I'd have been floundering and screaming. But the man opened his arms and legs in a gesture of perfect freedom and simply *soared*.

It was an amazing sight. A commentary explained that the man was plumetting at an incredible speed, but that high up it didn't look as if he was even moving. The world around him was as beautiful as he'd been promised. He inhabited it like a king – and suddenly it occurred to me that this was what Frankie had dreamt about when she was a little kid, all those years ago.

I wished I had my phone and could text her to switch on her telly. She ought to be watching this, I thought. Even I, who'd never had a flying dream, found myself captivated by this soaring figure. For the five minutes until the man pulled his cord, I felt as if I was flying too – and I wasn't scared. In fact, I loved it.

Afterwards, when the man had landed safely on the ground, I became my old, scared self again, who no way would go flying. But for five minutes back there I was another person – one who understood what Frankie had always said about freedom, flight and laughter going hand in hand.

The next day, when the shops opened again after their Christmas break, I was round at the Harbour Bookshop ordering a book on halo-jumping for Frankie with my Christmas money. It was an investment in her future, I told myself. And, in a strange way which I couldn't yet explain, it was an investment in my own.

The book took ages to arrive, although nobody knew why. The bookshop was embarrassed and I almost gave up going in and asking. Winter had almost turned to spring by the time it arrived. There were snowdrops in the garden and the lights were back on at Bradley Castle.

By now I'd got my phone back – though I was under strict instructions not to phone *the Bradley girl* on pain of death. It was the first thing I did, however, when I saw the lights. I rang and got no reply, then sent a text and phoned again, and kept on phoning until finally Frankie picked up.

It was such a surprise to hear her voice again that I couldn't think what to say. She asked how Christmas had been and I said the worst ever, and she said, 'Oh dear,' as if she couldn't think what to say either. I suggested meeting in Alf Resco's and she said it wouldn't be easy, but agreed to try.

I assumed the problem was her mother, the same as mine. But, when we did meet up, I was in for a shock. I had the halo book under my arm, I remember, wrapped in Christmas paper with Frankie's name on it. But I forgot all about it the moment I saw her. It wasn't just how thin she was. It was the wheelchair that took my breath away. Frankie in an electric wheelchair, propelling herself between the tables, everybody watching as she passed.

'What happened?' I said, imagining a skiing accident at the very least.

Frankie pulled a face. 'You mustn't laugh,' she said.
'Why would I do that?' I asked.

'Because it's funny,' Frankie said. 'I was queuing for the toilet.'

'You were *what*?' I said.

'It happened at school,' Frankie said. 'On the day we played that joke, would you believe? The toilet always had a slippery floor but, even so, I never expected to break my bones on it. Daddy was furious. You can just imagine. He said he was going to sue the school. At first everybody thought it was an ordinary break, but then something wasn't right with my X-rays and I ended up having to visit some fancy bone hospital in London. Then it all turned very complicated, which meant that I had to stay, and my parents moved up to our London house to be close to me.'

I hadn't known the Bradleys had a London house, but it didn't feel like the moment to say so.

'I'm really sorry,' I said instead, sticking the book on halo-jumping down the side of my chair because it wasn't the moment for extreme sports either. 'How long will you be in a wheelchair?'

Frankie didn't know, she said. We ordered our drinks and she told me all about her treatment. First she'd had to undergo radiotherapy to bring down the swelling in her leg and reduce the pain, then an operation to insert a metal plate, and then a punishing physiotherapy regime to get her leg working again. Even now she was still having it and, for weeks yet to come, she'd have to use the wheelchair every time she went out, just in case she broke anything else.

'Why would you do that?' I said, thinking that this sounded like another case of the Bradleys being overprotective.

'You might well ask,' Frankie said, and changed the subject, as if she'd had enough of Frankie Bradley. What about me, she wanted to know. Never mind boring old her, always going on about illnesses.

'What's been happening to you?' she said. 'And what about the joke? I never did find out – what happened that day when you got home from school?'

I filled her in, including the bit about our friendship being banned. 'And what about your mother?' I asked. 'How did *she* take it?'

Frankie pulled a face. She said that her mother had seen through it – or so she said – but that she'd gone along with the pretence to see how far Frankie would take it. In fact, she'd even kept the date with destiny at Exeter Cathedral, where she and Mum had had a terrible row over whose daughter was more to blame.

'Poor Mummy, she was furious,' Frankie said. 'The boys told me that, although she never said anything about it herself. She was too taken up, I suppose, with the unfolding drama of my accident. After all, I don't suppose the DSMCE counted for much compared to discovering that her daughter's cancer had moved into her bones.'

'That it's done what?' I said, staggering from one surprise to another.

Frankie flushed. She hadn't meant to say that. She didn't want to talk about it. She plainly hadn't meant to tell me. For a moment the two of us stared at each other in silence, then I dived down the side of my seat and pulled out the halo-jumping book.

Goodness only knows why I did that. Embarrassment maybe. Or shock. Certainly I wasn't thinking straight, otherwise I'd never have given a book on the most dangerous form of flying to a girl with diseased bones!

'For you,' I said.

'Thanks,' Frankie replied, looking like she didn't know what to do with it.

'You're going to love it,' I said. 'It's what you always dreamt of. Right up your street. And you could do it too. When you're better, of course. When they've fixed your bones. I'll sort it out for you. You've only got to ask.'

Some Facts About Cancer

After my ridiculous, embarrassed witterings, I went home and researched cancer on the Internet. According to the figures that I came up with, two hundred and seventy thousand people in the UK had been diagnosed with it in the past year, fifteen hundred of them children, and of that small number (given that the child population was eleven and a half million), about three hundred had died – twice as many boys as girls.

This was cause for celebration, I decided. Given the array of treatments that were available to a family with the Bradleys' money, the odds against Frankie being one of the hundred girls who would die out of eleven and a half million children were, I reckoned, pretty high.

I thought of emailing this information through to Frankie, to let her know how good her chances of survival were. But nobody so far had mentioned the possibility of death and I didn't want to be the one to put ideas into her head. Besides, what if my figures were wrong? I was feeling guilty enough already without handing out false hopes.

Guilt's the one thing above all others that stands out from that time. Guilt for being healthy while Frankie was sick. Guilt for being free while she was confined to a wheelchair. Guilt even for going to school while school, again, was off for her and she was going back and forth to the Royal South Hams, undergoing yet more chemotherapy.

I remember one Saturday afternoon, taking my guilt along to St Petrox's Church and trying to channel it into something useful. There's a sandbox at the front where you can put tiny lighted candles and say a prayer. I paid my twenty pence, stuck my candle in the sand and knelt on the stone floor, wanting to pray but unable to find the words. Outside a storm buffeted the church's walls. I imagined Frankie caught up in it, nothing to protect her but my silent vigil and the candle's tiny light.

'Why her?' I thought. 'Why not me? Why's life so unfair? Why do some people die young and others live long lives? In fact, why does anybody have to die? And what difference is a twenty-pence candle going to make? What difference does anything make?'

It was as close as I could manage to saying a

prayer – the best I could do in the circumstances. Afterwards I knelt on the floor, waiting for answers. When I didn't get them, I became angry. What I didn't realise at the time was that it's not only answers that matter. Questions matter just as much. Asking questions has this extraordinary way of bringing things to life.

Take that *why Frankie, not me?* question, for example. Up until that time, I'd always subconsciously believed that Frankie was a better person than me because she had a zest for life that I was sure I lacked. But did life really work like that? Was that really how people measured up? Did the active, sporty ones count for more than the people who only ever came up with ideas?

Of course they didn't. Ideas count for just as much as doing things. And dreaming things up is just another form of zest for life. You don't have to be an action girl to make a difference to the world. But if I hadn't asked that question I might never have known. And the difference made for me by a twenty-pence candle was that, in its light, I caught a glimpse of my worth.

The Joke Book

One of my better ideas, though I say it myself, was the joke book. I came up with it one night after crossing the river to see Frankie. It was during the time when she was having that second bout of chemotherapy. The flamingos had put together a flashy leather album full of photographs of everybody at her school, right down to the last caretaker and cat. The book was intended to cheer Frankie up, but I could tell from the way she showed it to me that all those photographs of healthy girls playing in tournaments, getting prizes and flicking back their lovely hair weren't having the desired effect.

It was after that that I came up with the joke book. I couldn't afford leather or anything like that – in fact, the best I could do was an old scrapbook with thick pages of rough paper, some of which had already been used. But in it I stuck copies of our mothers' DSMCE letters and a few jokes on medical matters that I'd cut out of magazines, some cartoons from the newspaper and a few silly photographs of people doing things that couldn't help but make you laugh.

Then, next time I sneaked up to see Frankie, I took it with me, suggesting that she might like to add jokes of her own, and we could pass it back and forth. Frankie loved the idea. In fact, later she told me that during the darkest days of her treatment, when she felt it would never end, the joke book became something of a lifeline.

Every day she tried to find something funny about her situation that could be put in. And nothing was off limits, it seemed, no matter how dark it might be. I remember a joke of Frankie's on the subject of baldness, and another about a surgeon with no hands. It felt sick laughing about things like that.

'But being sick *is* sick,' Frankie cracked. 'So when that's what you are, what else can you do?'

I agreed. I filled the book with jokes about Dartmouth men and boys who were in love with her, because the word was out about her having treatment again, which meant that she wasn't Little Miss Up-Herself any more but a tragic princess. Frankie must have liked that, because a rich new vein of princess jokes started springing up. It was as if her imagination had taken flight. Sometimes she'd even text or email the jokes to me, as if they couldn't wait. And sometimes, in the middle of the night, she'd phone for secret laughing sessions.

But it was a funny sort of laughter – hard and edgy – and one night it turned to tears, which came as no surprise.

'I just can't believe what's happening to me,' Frankie wept. 'Where did the old days go? Why can't I go back to school? Why do I have to keep going in for treatment? It's making no difference. I swear it's not. I want it stopped.'

Halo-Jumping

One Saturday afternoon I bumped into Diggers
Bradley in Dartmouth, and we began a friendship
that lasts to this day. I was strolling through town
when he pulled up beside me in one of the Bradley
family cars and invited me to get in. As half the people I knew in the world, including Bryony Rogers,
happened to be on the street that day, there was no
way I was going to say no. Up until then, I hardly
knew Diggers except to nod to, but I got in beside
him and he drove me round to the Dart Marina, and
ordered tea for two under the umbrella burners of
the Wildfire Bistro.

Afterwards I let it be known that Diggory Bradley
fancied me. It wasn't true, of course. I was just a little kid as far as he was concerned. The real reason
Diggers picked me up was because he wanted to
talk about his sister.

Apparently someone (Diggers wasn't mentioning

any names) had given Frankie a book on halo-jumping and, after weeks of ignoring it in favour of easier reads, she'd finally got round to it – with the result that she'd developed a violent obsession with doing a halo-jump herself. Not only that, but she seemed to think that the person who'd given her the book had promised to fix the whole thing up for her.

Diggers looked at me. I turned bright red, remembering what I'd said.

'You do know what I'm getting at here, don't you?' Diggers said.

'I meant when Frankie was better, not now,' I said.

'Well, you know what she's like,' Diggers said. 'Once she's got an idea, nothing's allowed to get in its way, so I thought you ought to be warned.'

I felt as if I was sinking. Halo-jumping just wasn't possible – if Frankie had read the book, she must know that.

'You have to be an expert sky-diver with hundreds of hours' experience in order to enrol on a halo-jumping course,' I said. 'And even to go sky-diving Frankie would need to be healthy and to have your parents' permission.'

'You try telling that to her,' Diggers said.

What had I done? I squirmed. 'I only meant to raise Frankie's spirits and give her something to take her mind off things. I didn't mean for her to take it seriously,' I said.

'Well, you can explain that to her when she phones you,' Digger said. 'Because she will. And soon, as well. You wait and see.'

Sure enough, that very night I got the call. I was to research training schools that taught halo-jumping and arrange for Frankie to enrol on a course as soon as her latest bout of chemotherapy was over. She would pay for it, of course. I wasn't to worry about that. And, while we were on the subject, I wasn't to worry about her parents either, because she'd sort them out, and her stupid, negative brothers, and Dr Herbert and anybody else who seemed to think it was a bad idea.

I'd seen Frankie in determined mode before, but never quite like this. Saying no was a total waste of time. And yet I had to try.

'I can't. You can't. I won't,' I said.

'You will,' she said. 'I can. *I've got to.*'

I didn't like that 'got to'. It smacked of obsession, which was the word Diggers had used, preceded by 'violent', which was another word I didn't like.

'Halo-jumping is for healthy men and women,' I said, taking a deep breath. 'It's for people with hundreds of hours of sky-diving under their belts, not for sick girls with breakable bones who've never even jumped out of a plane.'

There was no other way to say it, so I gave it to Frankie straight. And of course she got mad at me.

'You promised!' she exploded. 'You're the one who set me up for this. If you break your word and refuse to help *I'll never speak to you again!*'

She meant it too. You could hear the cold steel in her voice. There was something desperate in the way she spoke, as if her life hung in the balance.

'I would if I could,' I muttered pathetically. 'Believe me. But—'

She cut me off. Two days later, the joke book arrived in the post addressed to 'A False Ex-Friend — She Knows Who She Is'. Inside I found a note which read, 'I've had enough of you and your negativity, and I've had enough of your stupid book. Don't ever send it back. Here's one sick girl, with breakable bones, who *NEVER WANTS TO HEAR YOUR JOKES AGAIN.*'

I stuck the book in the drawer under my bed where all the clothes I never wear are kept. Diggers phoned, having got wind of what had passed between us. But not even he could comfort me.

'I feel so helpless,' I said. 'Frankie says I'm a false ex-friend, and she's right. I am.'

Diggers told me not to be so stupid.

'You're a real friend,' he said. 'Anyone can see

that. Even Mummy, for all her complaining about you. And you're not an ex. You're still a friend, no matter what Frankie says. You're not like some girls who think they've done their bit just because they've visited a couple of times. Frankie only has to have an off day and raise her voice and she doesn't see them again. But you stick by her through everything, and she knows that, no matter what she says.'

Good old Diggers! I was grateful for that, even though it didn't make much difference as far as Frankie getting in touch. Silence reigned between us and, after that, Diggers was the only Bradley I ever heard from, arranging to meet me every time there was anything he thought I ought to know about his sister. We'd sit outside the Wildfire Bistro and have coffee together. Why people thought George was the gorgeous one, I didn't know. Still don't, to be honest.

Diggers reckoned that it was the cancer making Frankie difficult these days. It wasn't the real her speaking; it was the illness.

But I didn't buy that. 'Something's changed,' I said. 'The real her is turning into someone else. It's not that Frankie's being difficult. It's that something's happening inside. Not in her body. Not even in her mind. But in her self. And I don't know what.'

Book Four

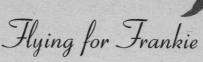

Flying for Frankie

I remember that conversation. It's always stuck in my mind. And I remember the night afterwards too, when I couldn't sleep for thinking about the process that was turning a plucky, lively girl into one who, I knew in my heart, was worrying about dying. Because that's what this was all about. The cold steel in Frankie's voice. The sense of something happening inside. Of the real her becoming someone else.

Even the violent obsession with flying was to do with worrying about dying. Deep down inside, I understood that Frankie was trying to prove to herself that there was nothing in life that couldn't be overcome. But it was death that she was struggling with, wasn't it? Death, not halo-jumping, that had her in this strange, obsessive state.

I longed to do something for Frankie, to put her mind at rest. But there were some things you could do for people, I reckoned, and others that you couldn't. Some things, in fact, that you couldn't even contemplate – and taking away their fear of death definitely came into that category.

Or so I thought.

I remember, some time during that night, turning on the radio to try and get myself off to sleep. Some man was going on about climbing a mountain with his dying father who hadn't been strong enough to complete the climb, leaving the son to finish it for him. I was deeply touched by what he said. The man was old and frail and had had to turn back, but at least he'd tried. No one had said he couldn't do it. No one had stood in his way, and it was wrong of me to stand in Frankie's way.

When I awoke next day, I knew that I'd got to get Frankie flying – even if the effort failed. In my break at school, I went on the Internet and researched halo-jumping training courses. To begin with it looked as if all the sky-diving schools that ran them were in Spain and California, but then, to my utter astonishment, I discovered one located on the far side of Dartmoor.

Taking this as a sign that I was doing the right thing, I reserved Frankie a flying voucher for a one-day introduction course, which would give her five hours' ground training and a small jump with an instructor. It wasn't halo-jumping, but at least it was a start. I ticked the boxes saying that Frankie was over eighteen and in perfect health. No to asthma. No to epilepsy. No to diabetes. No to heart conditions and, God forgive me, recent operations.

Then, once Frankie's name was down, I voice-mailed her to say what I'd done. How it was going to be achievable, especially given that Frankie's chemotherapy still wasn't over, I'd no idea. But, when she rang that night, that was the last thing on her mind.

She was over the moon, and sorry for the way she'd treated me. She'd known all along that I would make it happen, she said. She'd known that she could trust me. Once again I was the best friend in the world.

I pointed out I hadn't paid for anything and Frankie said she'd get that sorted. I also pointed out she'd have trouble persuading the sky-diving school to take her when they saw how young she was; that getting transport to the airfield might prove difficult, given how remote it was; and that I didn't see how her parents could fail to find out, or the hospital, given that she was still going in two days a week for treatment.

But nothing I said put Frankie off. As far as she was concerned, the whole thing was a done deed.

With a flight in sight, she announced that she now had something to work towards, making the treatment worthwhile. Getting better had a purpose. It had an end point – and unspoken between us was the fact of that end point not being death.

Three days before Frankie's flight, however, with everything booked and paid for, and transport arranged, Frankie pulled out. Of course, I'd hoped that this would happen but, when it did, sadness overwhelmed me.

'Thank God,' I said, when Frankie phoned in tears to say she wasn't well enough. 'You've seen reason.' What she didn't know was that I was in tears too.

Frankie was offended, but nothing had prepared me for how upset I'd be. If Frankie's death sentence had been announced, I couldn't have been more distressed. I lay awake for hours that night, her words running through my mind.

'So much for thinking positive,' she'd said. 'Some things are impossible. I've just got to accept that fact. No one can fight against them – Charis, I'm *really* scared.'

Somewhere towards morning, I turned on the radio to take my mind off things, only to get a repeat of that interview with the man who'd climbed a mountain with his dying father. It's like that on the radio – they're always repeating things. The man said he didn't know why he'd carried on when his father had had to stop. But he supposed he'd somehow felt as if, by finishing off the task, he could earn back his father's health. Maybe he'd felt guilty for being young and healthy while his dad was old and ill. Or maybe he'd carried on in the face of the helplessness we all feel when confronted by death.

And that was the moment when I knew that I'd have to fly in Frankie's place. Like that heroic son, I'd have to do it for her. I'd have to overcome my fear of flying (oh my God – *my fear of flying*) in order for Frankie to overcome her fear of death.

Long after the man had gone, I lay in bed thinking about what he'd said. Flying for Frankie was every bit as ridiculous as climbing a mountain for a dying old man, but it had made sense then, and I'd no doubt that it could make sense again. Next morning I phoned Frankie while my mind was still made up. When I said I'd make the flight on her behalf, there was silence down the line.

'Are you there?' I said at last.

'Do you really mean it?' Frankie answered in a voice that seemed to come from miles away.

'I never meant anything more in my life,' I said.

'Then *thank you*,' Frankie said. 'And I owe you. I

won't forget.'

For the next couple of days nothing else existed, as far as I was concerned, except the awfulness of what I'd agreed to do. For someone who didn't even like standing on cliff edges, and had to brace herself to climb a tree to fix a pallet in her den, the idea of jumping out of a plane was off the scale in terms of terror.

When the day itself arrived, I didn't have to pretend to anybody that I was sick in order to get out of school. I *was* sick. Mum reckoned from my burning skin that I must have flu and said there was a lot of it around. She headed off for work telling me that Grandma was only through the wall if I needed anything, and I should drink lots of water and stay in bed.

As soon as Mum had gone, however, I was up. I had half an hour before Frankie's driver was meant to call and, in that time, I had to forge my school ID card to add a few years, write a letter supposedly from my mother giving her permission in case the ID card didn't work, and generally make myself look over eighteen by borrowing some of Mum's clothes, applying her make-up and trying something different with my hair.

Not that I succeeded on any of those fronts. When the doorbell rang, I was in a total state. My

ID card was a write-off, none of Mum's clothes fitted, I'd completely failed on the make-up front and my hair looked a mess.

Diggers gawped at the apparition that stood before him – and I gawped back. 'It's *you*,' I said. 'You're my transport.'

He pulled a face. 'It looks like neither of us can say no to Frankie.'

We sneaked off quietly so that Grandma wouldn't hear. Then down the road in Diggers' car we talked through everything that was meant to be taking place. Today would be difficult, we both agreed, and tonight wasn't going to be much better, coming back late, unable to explain where we'd been all day.

'What have I got myself into?' I asked out loud.

'What have we both got ourselves into?' Diggers replied.

'*I'm* the one who's going flying,' I said.

'No, you're wrong there. When they refuse you, because you're obviously too young, *I'm* the one who'll be going flying,' Diggers said.

He shivered. I'd always thought those Bradley boys were up for anything, but he didn't look very happy.

'How do you feel about sky-diving?' I said.

'How do you think? I'm terrified,' Diggers answered. 'But not half as terrified as I am of telling

Frankie we didn't go through with it.'

Having wasted time talking, we drove out of town in a hurry, late already and with a long way to go. Diggers wasn't exactly the best of drivers. All the way up through the winding, deep lanes between Dartmouth and Totnes his car veered from one side of the road to the other as he talked to me, turning his head as if he'd forgotten he was at the wheel.

I felt sick long before we reached the sky-diving school. Most of the way I had my eyes closed. 'How much longer?' I kept saying. But the answer was always, 'Ages yet.'

At Buckfastleigh, we stopped in a petrol station to fortify ourselves with sandwiches that Diggers insisted I eat, no matter how I felt. Then we hit a stretch of dual carriageway and I closed my eyes again. Finally – mercifully – the roar of traffic died behind us. I opened my eyes to find us winding along a new series of deep lanes buried between high hedges. Dartmoor rose before us and soon the last of the hedges gave way to miles of open, rolling heath.

The road was single-track, but Diggers continued to speed. It was a shame, because it would have been nice to savour the views. Only when we reached the track to the airfield, way over the other side of Dartmoor, did we finally slow down.

'We haven't made bad time. We're only half an hour late,' Diggers announced in triumph.

I allowed myself a small groan, somewhere between relief that we were alive and fear of what lay ahead. The track cut between steep banks, then suddenly opened out and our destination appeared in the form of an airstrip and a couple of small planes.

We had arrived. Ahead of us stood a hangar surrounded by people in jumpsuits hauling parachutes about, a succession of hut-like shops and offices, a snack bar, a bunkhouse and a toilet block.

We pulled into a car park, which was full to capacity, all the other participants on the course having already arrived. I looked at Diggers. He looked at me. Feeling sick, I got out of the car. We walked towards the hangar and I was embarrassingly aware of my appearance letting me down. No way did I look eighteen. In fact, no way did I look like anyone who might be serious about taking my first sky-dive.

A man came towards us in full flying gear, including boots, gloves, goggles and a bright blue crash helmet. He pushed the goggles up onto the helmet and asked what he could do for us. I explained that I was booked in for the day's introductory course and he didn't need to say a word for me to know what was coming next. He looked me up and down and his face said it all. I'd have to sort myself out in the office, he said. They were the ones who'd arrange my refund. No way could I fly with them. My mother's forged letter of permission made no difference. Nor did my equally forged ID card. The man refused to even look at them.

I was too young and that was that. Even Diggers, stepping in to say he'd do the day instead, was deemed unacceptable. It was so embarrassing. All the other people stopped what they were doing and listened in, smiling superior smiles because they happened to be older than us.

It was particularly galling for Diggers. I'm sure that's why he got so mad. Was the instructor telling him, he shouted, his face bright red, that after travelling all this way we were being turned away? Was that fair? Was it even good business? Surely not. In fact, as an exercise in customer relations, it sucked!

But Diggers's anger got him nowhere. The school reserved the right to turn down anyone they deemed unfit and, by the time Diggers had finished giving vent to his feelings, we were lucky to even get a refund.

In the end, we sloped back to the car. Diggers revved the engine and drove off in a cloud of blue exhaust fumes.

'Would you mind driving more slowly this time?'

I dared to ask.

'I'm sorry. You should have said before. I didn't know my driving was a problem,' Diggers snapped.

We drove home in silence and very slowly, as if Diggers was making a point. He must have been relieved somewhere deep inside that he didn't, after all, have to make that jump, but it certainly didn't show.

Far from being relieved, however – and much to my surprise – I was disappointed. I kept telling myself that I'd been let off the hook, but I'd look up at the sky and wonder what it was like up there. If only I'd been older, I told myself, or more quick-witted or determined, I could have been up there right now. There were wonders beyond imagining out there in the world. And the sky was one of them and I'd missed my chance.

Telling Frankie what had happened, though, was worse than anything else. I thought at least she'd give me credit for having tried. But it didn't work like that. Frankie phoned halfway home, to see how everything was going, and when she heard what had happened – or, to be precise, what hadn't – she totally lost it.

'You never meant to fly, did you?' she shrieked down the phone. 'The whole thing was for show. If you'd meant it to happen, you'd have made sure that it did. But then that's you all over, Charis. You're all talk and no action. So why am I surprised? I should have known. You wanted out from the word go – *and out's what you got.'*

At this point in the rant, Diggers took the phone off me. He shouldn't have done it because he was the driver, but he didn't let the small matter of being behind the wheel come between him and a full expression of his feelings. Did Frankie know what she'd asked of us? he demanded. Did she realise how hard we'd tried for her – how difficult the whole day had been, and how much trouble we'd risked getting into, at our respective schools, not to say anything of back at home?

In the end, Diggers pulled up on the roadside and they had a full-scale argument, hurling insults at each other. All his pent-up feelings about being humiliated at the training school came pouring out. Maybe his pent-up feelings about his sister too, for being sick and always getting all the fuss and attention. Who knows?

When we got back to Dartmouth, the two of us went our separate ways with scarcely a word to each other apart from *thanks* on my part and *goodbye* on his. I returned to my bed without Grandma noticing anything amiss, and I worked at my flu symptoms until Mum and Dad came in.

But that night I lay awake, thinking about what Frankie had said and wondering if there was any truth in it. Had I really engineered the situation so that I wouldn't have to fly? I told myself I hadn't, but perhaps I had. Perhaps subconsciously I'd had the whole thing planned.

One thing was for certain, though – I'd let Frankie down.

I'd set out to prove that things like fear and death could be overcome but I'd gone and done the opposite.

I lay there in the darkness, feeling overwhelmed. There really were some things you could do for people and others that you couldn't, just the way I'd always thought. I was so helpless. I felt so small.

And yet there *were* things I could do, even though I didn't know it yet. And funnily enough, it took Judith Mason to show me that.

The Night Nurse

After the sky-diving incident, Frankie and I trod around each other cautiously for a while. Neither of us wanted to fall out, but neither quite trusted the other any more. We were still friends, but there's no way I'd have gone sneaking up in the night, or she'd have phoned me in the early hours of morning, to share her secrets. She retreated into herself and I did the same, texting bright, friendly messages – 'I'm doing this', 'I'm doing that' – but never going any deeper.

Then, one Saturday, I decided enough was enough and went up to see her. I didn't expect Mrs Bradley to let me in but, much to my surprise, she did. Perhaps she'd realised by now that I wasn't the monster she'd once thought. Perhaps Diggers had spoken up on my behalf. Or perhaps she could tell how pleased Frankie would be to see me, and reckoned I might be useful to keep her entertained.

After that, I went up most weekends and found Frankie with her mother, watching telly, reading, doing a bit of cooking or sitting out on the terrace, thumbing through magazines. Poor old Frankie – her latest bout of chemotherapy was over, but she still wasn't back at school and it was obvious how bored she was. Secretly, I blamed her parents. They'd got her all wrapped up in cotton wool. She couldn't do this, couldn't do that. The list was endless. If Frankie seemed listless, it was their fault, not hers.

But one day when I went up I began to see things in a different light. The weather was really lousy, a storm was blowing in from the sea and perhaps I should have stayed at home. When I arrived, Frankie was in bed, having what Mrs Bradley called one of her *off days*. She told me to go up, but said that if Frankie was asleep it might be a good idea not to disturb her.

Upstairs, I found the blinds drawn, the television on, the sound turned down and Frankie, eyes wide open, staring at the ceiling. When she saw me, she turned up the telly without saying a thing, and we sat side by side and channel-surfed.

Outside rain lashed against the side of the house and I caught glimpses of lightning between the slats in the blinds. But Frankie didn't notice. She dozed on and off and only when I got up to leave did she rouse herself.

'Goodbye,' she said. 'Thanks for coming. I'm sorry for being so out of it. Blame the medication.'

I went downstairs, wondering what she meant about medication. In my sad little brain, I'd equated Frankie coming off her latest course of chemotherapy with her being better. It was crazy, I know, but desperate people see things in a desperate light – and I was desperate to see Frankie as someone on the road to recovery.

I said I'd better leave and, because the weather was so bad, Frankie's mother drove me to the ferry. I remember wanting to ask about the medication but not being able to face it. When we arrived at the river, we found it seething like a witch's brew and all crossings suspended until further notice. It was Easter time, but it might as well have been midwinter.

Frankie's mother drove me back to Bradley Castle, saying I'd have to stay the night. I said I couldn't possibly, knowing that Mum would have a blue fit if she knew that Frankie and I were in touch again. But Mrs Bradley phoned on my behalf and, instead of being angry, Mum was fine. In fact, when Mrs Bradley handed me the phone, all Mum said was that I should have known better than to cross the river in this sort of weather.

That night Mrs Bradley put me in a guest bed-room full of African furniture, weavings and carved masks. It was hard to sleep with those eyeless faces staring down at me and the storm raging outside. Things were happening down the corridor too – lights being turned on and people moving about. Once Frankie cried out, and her voice sounded so plaintive that I sneaked out of bed and went to see if there was anything I could do to help.

When I got to Frankie's room, however, there was no way that I was needed, what with Frankie's parents leaning over her bed and a nurse in a blue uniform – a nurse, I mean *a nurse* – there too, plumping up Frankie's pillows and doing nurse-like things, such as bringing drinks and pills.

'Don't be frightened, sweetheart. You're all right,' I heard the nurse murmuring, and saw Frankie's parents – their eyes wide open like a pair of startled deer caught in headlights – nodding in agreement.

I slipped away, snatching a glimpse of a tight, tiny, distressed face that didn't look like Frankie. Next morning, when I went back, her room was empty but I could hear her in her bathroom. The storm outside was over and sunshine came pouring through the blinds. The balcony doors were ajar and I slipped outside. Here I stood looking down at the river, which was swollen with rain. Much to my surprise, I found myself crying. It was as if I knew something that morning that I hadn't allowed myself to know last night.

Behind me, I could hear someone – I assumed it was Frankie – crossing the bedroom. I tried to muffle my sobs, but whoever it was came through the balcony doors and stood beside me. I turned my head away, reckoning I couldn't have been more embarrassed if I'd tried. But at least they didn't touch me or attempt to speak until I'd pulled myself together. Then I felt a hand on my shoulder and a voice said, 'Don't be frightened, sweetheart,' just as it had done to Frankie last night.

It was the night nurse. I turned towards this blue-uniformed stranger, not quite knowing what to say – only to find myself staring into the face of Judith Mason.

Judith Mason.

'You!' I said.

'Charis!' she replied. 'So you're the friend who stayed the night. I'm so sorry. This isn't easy, is it? *Death never is.*'

Later, when Judith came off her shift, we went down to the river together. The ferries were running again and we crossed together in her car. Neither of us mentioned the words that had inadvertently slipped off Judith's tongue, but they hung between us all the same.

'I feel so helpless,' I said at last. 'I'm not like you. I'm not a nurse. I'm not Frankie's mother or her father. There's nothing I can do to help.'

Judith smiled at that. Her eyes were huge and full of sympathy. I'd never really looked at them before. Never seen the kindness in them, shining like a lighthouse keeping danger at bay.

'Don't kid yourself,' she said. 'There's everything that you can do. For starters, just by being here you're doing something that counts. By standing alongside Frankie and being her friend. And there'll be other things as well. Keep your eyes open, Charis. Life's a funny old business. It may seem without hope. But you never know what'll turn up next.'

Kite Flying

April was a busy month on the gardening front. There were potatoes that needed to go in, broad beans that were coming up and onions to be sown, along with climbing beans, lettuces and winter greens. In the greenhouse, tiny tomato plants were sprouting yellow flowers. In the cold frame, cucumber seedlings needed watering every night.

Not only that, but the lawn kept needing cutting, roses needed feeding, daffodils and tulips awaited dead-heading and the last of the winter weeds needed pulling up to make room for all the summer flowers – poppies, lupins, delphiniums and the rest.

Over that month, every spare minute when Judith wasn't nursing Frankie she was in our garden, bringing it to life. At the same time, she was teaching Dad how to do it for himself. Under her tuition, he was a changed man.

'Watching seeds coming up that you've planted

yourself is a wonderful experience,' he exclaimed, to everyone's surprise. 'They're tiny miracles, each and every one of them. What they do when they get mixed up with soil is a miracle too. And the soil is wonderful. It smells alive. I can't think how else to describe it. Why, if I'd had Judith to teach me all those years ago when my poor old father tried, I'd have grown up with a completely different attitude to gardening.'

Mum wasn't impressed, no matter what Dad said. And, out of solidarity, neither was I. But, despite myself, my attitude to Judith was softening. It was hard to think of her as a monster when I saw the way she cared for Frankie. And it was hard to carry on being cross all the time when the garden looked like something off a 'Beautiful Devon' calendar.

Summer was opening up all around us and the harshness of winter was a thing of the past. The days were getting longer, the air was warm, birds sang in the trees and seagulls nested in the chimney pots. Grandma sat out in the garden, enjoying the sun. Even Mum was persuaded to come outside and enjoy it too, just so long as Judith Mason wasn't about.

The whole of Dartmouth was basking in the good weather, and up at Bradley Castle Frankie was basking in it too. Against all odds, her life was suddenly on the up. The dark shadow that had hung over her on that dreadful night of the storm seemed to have disappeared. I began to feel as if Judith had never mentioned the death word. It was as if even cancer couldn't withstand the onslaught of summer.

I remember one day in particular. I went up to the house to find George home from university for the weekend with some girlfriend and Diggers back from boarding school, trying to teach himself how to play the guitar. Mr Bradley was in his study, listening to a recording of his favourite racing-car engines, while Mrs Bradley was in the kitchen and Frankie was lounging on the sofa, working her way through a pile of magazines.

Everyone was indoors when they should have been outside. And, as if she thought so too, Judith suddenly came sweeping through the house like a whirlwind, gathering us all up and whisking us out into the garden. The sun was shining. The sky was blue. A light breeze was blowing – and that meant only one thing as far as she was concerned.

Kite flying.

I'll never forget that crazy afternoon. Lined up on the lawn was a row of kites that Judith had found in one of the garages. Frankie chose the big white box-shaped one made of tissue paper so thin that the sun shone through it. Her mother chose the butterfly. Her father homed in immediately upon the eagle. Diggers grabbed the superhero – I think it was meant to be Spiderman. I went for the dragon with the curly tail. And George: well, it was obvious – Gorgeous George had to have the red Ferrari!

At first, none of us could get our kites into the air because we didn't have the knack. But Judith soon sorted us out. She divided us into pairs and made one person in each pair hold the string and stand with their back to the wind, pulling and running backwards, while the other person tilted the kite at just the right angle and lifted it up.

Suddenly it was like watching a succession of planes taking off. One after another, as the breeze got under our kites, they soared into the air. At one point the whole lot of them were flying at the same time, which was wonderful until they got all tangled up and came crashing down.

But, tangled or not, it was the greatest fun. For a while we completely forgot ourselves. George forgot he had a girlfriend that he needed to impress. Frankie forgot that she hadn't had the energy for anything but the sofa. Judith forgot that she was meant to be a nurse, and I don't know what Diggers and I forgot, but we certainly had a good time.

Most remarkable of all, Frankie's parents completely and utterly forgot *themselves*. I'd never seen them like this before. For one short, crazy afternoon they weren't just putting on a show for the world to see, or smiling for the sake of it, like they usually did. Running up and down the lawn, struggling to keep their kites airborne, they laughed and shouted as they watched them soaring overhead.

I knew that what I was seeing was the real them, with everything else stripped away. And the others knew it too. Frankie, George and Diggers – at one point they all forgot their kites and watched their parents in amazement.

When the last kite fell from the sky, everything returned to normal. The kites were badly in need of untangling, but who in the Bradley family was going to bother when there were people around who could do it for them? George and his girlfriend headed back to their love nest in his bedroom. Mr and Mrs Bradley returned to what they'd been doing before. Frankie headed back to her magazines and even Judith disappeared.

That left only me and Diggers. We gave a moment's thought to doing the untangling, but then laziness got the better of us and we headed off together for the summer house.

'At least no one had to risk their life this afternoon,' Digger said, remembering our sky-diving attempt.

'Or doctor their ID,' I said.

'Or forge a letter from their mother, granting permission,' Diggers said.

We both laughed. I remember wishing that I was old enough for Diggers to fall in love with me. I blushed at the thought of it, looking out of the summer-house window to where Judith had reappeared and was busy untangling the kites.

My heart went out to her. Good old Judith. Everything we'd done this afternoon had been because of her. Everything we'd seen and laughed at and achieved. She was the one who'd dragged us outside. The one who'd found the kites and shown us how to fly them. But then, she was always bringing things to life, whether they be people, flowers or kites.

Perhaps Mum had got her wrong and perhaps I had too.

The Poem with No Title

After that, I remember us going through a sort of golden phase. The days were long, warm and continued to be shadow-free. The joke book came out again and started making its journey back and forth between us. Frankie even went back to school one day a week and the other days were open house up at Bradley Castle.

The change in Frankie's parents' attitude was remarkable. In the early days of her illness, no one had been allowed up because of germs. But now all sorts of people came on an almost daily basis. It wasn't just the flamingos who were welcome, or Mrs Bradley's special friends. One time I found John Bepp up there, playing the piano and singing Frankie the sorts of songs that had driven our mothers out of the choir. And another time, to my total astonishment, I went up and found my loud and uncouth brother teaching Diggers how to play blues guitar.

My brother Damo – how weird was that?

But then, another time, I even found Mum up there. To my astonishment, she and Mrs Bradley had buried their differences and decided they'd try their hands at being friends.

I remember one particular day when we were all there – the whole lot of us. Mum and Mrs Bradley were making lunch. Mr Bradley was playing tennis with my dad, of all people. Diggers, who seemed to be spending more time home from school these days than at it, was playing the guitar with Damo. George was on a sunbed on the lawn, topping up his tan. Frankie and I sat making daisy chains as if we were little kids again. Even a couple of neighbours dropped in.

There was a magic about that day. After lunch, Frankie persuaded her father to boat the two of us round to Castle Cove. She didn't explain about it being our special place, but simply said that we wanted to collect shells and it was the best place around.

I worried all the way that Mr Bradley might want to stay and would then discover our den. But Frankie must have briefed him very carefully because he dropped us on the beach, along with a couple of fold-up chairs, in case we got tired, and a hamper of food, in case we got peckish, and then left.

Everything was laftish that afternoon. Everything was mesmiritious. We hadn't used those words for ages, but no others would do. It was like coming home after living abroad. Speaking one's mother tongue after being among strangers.

At one point, Frankie went round touching everything. There was something almost ritualistic about the way she did it, one thing at a time. Nothing was missed out. I watched, her head slightly bowed and eyes half-closed, as if she was storing the things she touched inside her head.

Before her father came back, we ate chocolate brownies and toasted each other in mango juice. Then Frankie announced that she wanted to recite a poem that she'd recently made up. I was surprised, because I hadn't known that Frankie was interested in poetry. She said she wasn't, but that the words had written themselves.

'It doesn't have a title,' she said. 'But I'll think of one later. This is how it goes . . .'

She closed her eyes. I fixed my own on the sea beyond the cove. An oystercatcher flew overhead in a flash of black and white. Waves broke against the shoreline, murmuring an accompaniment to Frankie's voice.

What is this place?
Will I return?
Will I come back to fly across
its grass-green hills, caught up
in dreams of freedom, flight and laughter
by a wind that looks like rain
but I can't see, and pins me down
and yet I'm free?
This place where, for a few, short, laughing
minutes I was truly me.
And was it just a dream,
or was there more?
Was something out there
beyond my grasp, waiting
like a gift of joy or sorrow
to be delivered at my door?
A lifetime's joys and sorrows
to be unpacked and toyed with,
yes, but possessed, no.
Impossible to say.
For the dream has passed now.
I'm awake.
Already it's too late.

When I read the poem later (in my joke book, of all places, where Frankie had written it out, right at the back), I saw that Frankie never had given it a title. Why one notices insignificant things like that, I really don't know. And nor do I know what I feel about that poem. All I know is that I read it, then shut the book and didn't want to think about it any more.

Candles Again

Death was in the air after that. People carried on as if it wasn't, but it was always there, lurking in the background like an uninvited guest at one of Mrs Bradley's lunches.

The person I didn't expect it to take, though, was Grandma. I came home from school one day to find that what we'd all thought was nothing but a nasty cough was, in fact, pneumonia. It came as an extraordinary shock. And so did the fact that, even though she was rushed straight into hospital, Grandma got worse instead of better.

I remember the silence in the house, which replaced the energy Grandma usually generated. A terrible nothingness hung over us all. Life without Grandma was unthinkable. None of us knew what to do or say.

Grandma's health had weathered the winter with all its draughts and gales – and yet a week in hospital did for her. The nurses said it would have happened anyway, even if there hadn't been an infection on the ward. They said Grandma's lung had collapsed and then her heart had given out.

The whole thing was over very quickly. Once it was obvious the way things were heading, Mum got me out of school, picked up Damo and drove the two of us to the hospital. Dad was there already, crouched over Grandma's bed. But before the rest of us arrived she'd already gone.

The funeral was a bigger affair than any of us expected. The Johncoxes turned up in memory of the old days and the Shropshire relatives were there too – the ones we'd done the van swap with – as well as all sorts of relatives that I hadn't even known existed.

After the service, Mum held a buffet lunch in Grandma's side of the house. I helped take round sandwiches and cakes, my ears ringing with stories of a grandma I'd never known. A board was set up with photos going right back to her babyhood. Someone had got hold of a family tree. Someone else had photos in a rolling slide show on their laptop.

By the time that everybody left, driving out of Dartmouth saying, now that Grandma – the last of her generation – had gone, we must be sure to keep in touch, Dad, Mum, Damo and I were exhausted. A strange atmosphere hung over the house. Dad went off somewhere, nursing memories that he didn't want to share with anyone, not even us. Mum wandered about in a daze, trying to take in the fact that there'd be no more knocking on walls or Grandma sweeping through unannounced.

In an act of togetherness that was rare, Damo and I told Mum to go and have a rest while we did the clearing up. But even when the last cup and saucer had been washed, and the last chair put back in place, the strange atmosphere remained.

I wanted to talk to Frankie about it, but she wasn't available. I phoned her mobile but got no reply. Phoned the house and got no reply. Phoned again later and got Mrs Bradley, who told me that Frankie was in bed. It had been her treatment day, she said.

'What treatment?' I asked, thinking that she'd finished with all that.

Looking back, I can't remember exactly what Mrs Bradley said. But afterwards I took myself off to St Petrox's Church in a state of total panic. The golden days were over. Even I could see that. Obviously one small candle, lit back in January, hadn't been enough.

That afternoon, I lit a whole pile of candles, filling the sandbox and not caring that I didn't have enough twenty pences to pay for them. God would understand, I told myself. He'd know this was an emergency. I absorbed their warmth and light, though feeling cold inside.

When I look back, I marvel that I grasped so late how very ill Frankie was. Ever since that day when Judith Mason had let the death word slip, I'd known the score and yet I'd deliberately chosen to be blind. Even when Frankie recited her poem, I'd refused to recognise what it was saying.

Now I knelt on the floor, staring into nothing, thinking about the cancer in Frankie's bones, which hadn't gone – of course it hadn't – just because the summer had come along. Where was it now? Had it grown? And by how much? And what difference was Frankie's treatment making?

I felt a fool for having acted as if the whole thing had gone away. On numerous occasions there'd been the chance to question Frankie's mother, or even Judith Mason. But I never had. I'd never pushed it. I'd told myself I was no good at understanding the way that bodies worked. But the truth was that I hadn't *wanted* to understand.

And perhaps Frankie hadn't wanted me to either. Perhaps it had been easier hiding behind lines of verse than coming out and saying that she was still scared of death.

'Dear God,' I prayed. 'Save Frankie's life. Don't let her die. And help us to be honest with each other. Help us to stop running. Nothing hidden any more, nothing secret, no pretence. Just give us openness.'

I didn't only pray this in St Petrox's. As if wanting to make sure that God had heard, I prayed it all over Dartmouth. I prayed in the Catholic church. Prayed in the little Anglican church in Kingswear, and again in the big town church, St Saviour's, in the centre of town. I prayed in the Baptist church, the Friends' Meeting House, the Salvation Army citadel and the Philadelphian church.

Then, just to be on the safe side, I took my prayer to the lamp posts of Dartmouth, tying ribbons round them on Frankie's behalf. No one, to this day, knows that the secret Dartmouth ribbon-tying person was me, or that the ribbons were prayers.

Finally, having exhausted all other avenues to God that I could think of, I wrote a prayer using a whole string of Castle Cove words, and buried it down there in a crack in the cliff face, telling myself that God was a God of cliffs and coves every bit as much as a God of churches, and could read prayers wherever I chose to put them.

Behind my actions, of course, was the hope that God was really out there, big and wise, a loving presence beyond the veil of ordinary life, seeing the things that happened and caring for people's lives. He could hear me. He could answer. It was in his power. And, if not, what else had Frankie got?

Openness

While the Bradley parents' world revolved around Frankie, Diggers had A levels to prepare for and George faced exams that determined whether or not he'd pass his first year at university. For both of them it must have been a complicated balancing act. Looking back, I don't know how they managed it. They came home almost every weekend, wanting to spend as much time as possible with their sister, but were always surrounded by books and papers. There'd be essays to write, coursework to prepare and deadlines hanging over them.

I felt sorry for them. I know Frankie did as well. I remember us sitting out on the top terrace one afternoon. Diggers was below us in the summer house with the door open, his work spread out around him, but George was indoors and had his windows closed, as if he was trying to pretend it wasn't sunny outside.

'It's just not fair,' said Frankie. 'Poor old them. Normally exams are the most important thing happening in this house and everything in our family revolves around them. But now the boys have to take a back seat to me being sick. They must feel sick themselves. Sick of revision and definitely sick of me for getting all the attention.'

It was the first time I'd heard Frankie admit how much life at Bradley Castle had changed because of her. But it wasn't just the people who had changed; it was the house itself. It smelt different. Looked different. And people used it in a different way. It wasn't just a showcase any more; it was a house with a whole new series of functions.

A couple of days after that conversation, for example, I arrived to find Frankie's bedroom being moved downstairs. A string of cleaning ladies and gardeners, under Mrs Bradley's supervision, were hauling down all Frankie's possessions, right to the last pair of shoes and teddy bear.

'What's going on?' I said.

Mrs Bradley explained that Frankie was being moved because of the increased amounts of time she was spending upstairs, away from the life of the family.

'This will be so much nicer,' she said. 'We're moving Frankie into the Snug, which is right at the heart of the house, so she'll always have her family round her and be in touch with what's going on. It also means that she can go in and out of the garden through the French windows whenever she wants, and she won't have all those awful stairs and corridors to negotiate.'

Everyone seemed to agree that the Snug was much nicer than Frankie's old bedroom – friendlier, cosier and with loads more sun. None of the rooms in Bradley Castle were exactly what I'd have called cosy, but after the Snug's heavy old furniture had been removed and Frankie's had replaced it, I could see what they were getting at. She and I spent hours together unpacking things. We were both exhausted long before we'd finished, and Mrs Bradley invited me to stay the night.

I thought how much things had changed since the first time I'd crossed the river in the night, when our friendship had been a terrible dark secret. I was still that same dreadful girl who'd set up Mrs Bradley to meet Prince Charles – the one who'd applauded her daughter's wig-removing antics – but now I'd been accepted as part of their family life.

That night I was even allowed to sleep on the fold-up sofa bed in the Snug instead of the guest bedroom full of African masks. Here Frankie and I watched television together until I fell asleep. I woke up later to find it still on. Frankie was awake in front of it, but her laptop was on too and she was typing.

When she saw my eyes open, she apologised for disturbing me. I remember a game show was on the telly, complete with a grinning host in a silver suit. Frankie asked if I wanted her to turn it off. I said she could do what she liked, and she left it on and returned to her typing. I lay watching it but not watching, if you know what I mean, and was just beginning to drop off to sleep again when Frankie suddenly climbed out of her bed and hauled her laptop over to me.

'Read this,' she said.

'What is it?' I said.

'Read it,' she said.

It was her Last Will and Testament. I stared at the words on the screen and my mouth went dry.

'Frankie,' I said, my heart hammering, 'are you really sure you want me to?'

Frankie didn't look at me, but said to go ahead. Not knowing how to get out of it, I started reading. On the possessions front, Diggers was to get Frankie's laptop, CDs, DVDs, computer games and watch. George was to get her phone, her iPod and her books. Her make-up (which she said was really expensive and to be treated with respect) was to be shared out among the flamingos. I was to get the clothes that she'd tried to give me ages ago but I'd never taken. Her father was to get her silver fountain pen and locket. And her mother got everything else, including her jewellery, which she could sell, if she wanted, and donate the proceeds to cancer charities.

I had to stop when I got this far and take a breath.

'You haven't finished. Carry on,' Frankie said.

I stared at her and she stared back. I'd prayed for openness but this was more than I'd bargained for.

'*Read it,*' Frankie said again, and I carried on. I had no choice.

Having disposed of her belongings, Frankie's Will moved on to her funeral arrangements. She was to be cremated, she said, and her ashes scattered in Castle Cove. She wanted the word *mesmiritious* to be spelt out on her coffin in blue flowers with silver leaves. There were to be jokes at her funeral, and if people didn't laugh she'd take offence. I could even read from the joke book, if I liked, and she wanted her father to read out her poem.

That was as far as I got. There was a page more of this stuff, but I pushed the laptop away. I was lost for words. Tears of anger pricked my eyes. This was so unnatural. So totally obscene. Here we were, two girls barely in our teens. We shouldn't have to be talking about things like this. It was *disgusting*.

Suddenly I didn't want openness any more. I didn't want honest talk between friends. Prayers were dangerous things, I decided. You had to think very carefully before saying them, just in case they got answered. Better to say nothing than to get the wrong thing.

The House on Above Town

Those were Difficult Days – with a capital D for 'difficult' and another one for 'days'. As if I didn't have enough to worry about on the Frankie front, I had trouble at home. Now that Grandma was dead, things were different in ways that none of us could have anticipated. For starters we missed Grandma (I mean, we missed her loads, and that's something that came as a surprise – at least it did to me). Then, instead of feeling as if it was ours because we'd inherited it, the house felt weird and empty. Dad was always off somewhere, crying in corners, which came as a shock because I'd never seen him like that before. Damo was there less and less, so he almost didn't seem to live with us any more. Even Mum, who for years had longed for a house without Grandma, let alone more space, trailed around the place as if the heart had gone out of it and it wasn't home any more.

Weeks after the funeral, we were still living cramped in our side of the house, the doors firmly closed between us and Grandma's part. It was as if her ghost had taken up residence next door and was holding us at bay. I'd walk past her kitchen window and swear I could see her there, even though I knew it was only a play of light on the glass. Or I'd see her chair – the one she always sat in – empty and abandoned, and something would go through me like a knife.

It was really creepy. No one had to tell us that Grandma's side of the house was out of bounds. It was simply something that we felt. So, instead of taking up the extra space we'd always dreamt about, we started talking about moving house.

It was Dad who started it. I'd have expected him, of all of us, to be the one who wanted to hang on to the house, while Mum wanted to sell it. But, surprisingly, it was the other way round.

'Enough of tears,' Dad suddenly announced one day. 'We can't carry on like this, living in half a house as if we have no right to the rest of it. What we need is a new start.'

Apparently, the perfect opportunity had already presented itself. It came in the form of a house on Above Town, currently rented out as a holiday home by one of the bosses at Dad's work. This boss had approached Dad, knowing that he'd inherited what, by anybody's standards, was an interesting property, wondering whether he'd care to do a swap.

'What do you mean, a *swap*?' Mum said, sniffing the way she always did when Dad mentioned any of his bosses whom she'd always distrusted because of how much money they earned.

'I mean that we buy the Above Town house and Henry Askew buys ours,' Dad said. 'Ours is older and a bit run down, but it still has lots of original features, which is what he's after. Ours is bigger of course, but his property is modern and *very* smart. And, being on Above Town, it has one of Dartmouth's best addresses. And, besides, it's got fantastic views.'

Dad knew what he was talking about because he'd been to see the house already. It was a bargain, he reckoned, and one we should snap up, not least because his boss was offering it for sale privately, which meant no money wasted on estate agents' fees and no chain to hold up the sale.

'If we can agree on this,' Dad said, 'once the conveyancing has been done, we could move fairly quickly.'

He was really excited at the prospect, but Mum was angry. She didn't trust Henry Askew, she said.

Of all the directors at Dad's company, she'd always thought he was the dodgiest. She didn't trust any of them, but Henry Askew in particular, with his flash cars and his yacht, never did a thing except for his own advancement.

Besides, she added, she knew the place Dad meant and he had to be crazy. The Above Town property might have a good location, looking down over the Dartmouth rooftops to the river and out to sea. But it didn't have the character of our house and wasn't half as big either – especially with the two sides put together.

'We've been waiting years for this,' she said, 'all cooped up, imagining what it would be like to finally open the doors and spread out. And you're not taking this away from us. No way are we moving into that poky little house!'

Dad took us round to see the house, but Mum wouldn't budge. I loved it immediately but was too scared to say so. It was built on split levels, had enormous windows that filled it with sunshine, polished oak flooring and views from every room. How anybody could bear to part with it, I couldn't imagine. Maybe our house was bigger, but who would give up all this wonderful light?

When we got home, however, the battle began in earnest. Mum said that, apart from the view, the

Above Town house had little going for it.

'I can see what Henry Askew would get out of this,' she said. 'But not us.'

Dad insisted that the Above Town house was bigger than it appeared. Mum said it was characterless. Dad said it had character – it was just that she didn't have the taste to see it.

Mum got mad when Dad said that, and even madder when he added that the trouble with her was that she couldn't abide change. 'You've got no spirit of adventure,' he said.

'That's rich,' she spat back, 'coming from a man who's lived with his mother all his life. Spirit of adventure, indeed! You're being conned – can't you see it?'

Dad said that, far from being conned, he'd had the houses valued and the deal was in our favour, no doubt about that. It wouldn't lose us money, he said, and, as he was always careful with the pennies, we could trust his judgement, which was that the Above Town house was as good as cash in the bank.

Mum laughed at that. It was a hard laugh and I didn't like it. She said that the Above Town house didn't even have a garden, just a bit of decking and a couple of tubs, and how would Dad – not to say anything of his pal Judith Mason – cope with that?

'There's no need to be nasty,' Dad said.

'I'm not being nasty,' Mum retorted, 'just practical. Someone's got to be. I mean, there are all sorts of things you haven't thought about. The garden's only one of them. Like, given how few bedrooms there are, where's everybody meant to sleep?'

At this point Damo – who had remained silent until now – informed us that he'd been offered a job in Plymouth and had decided to take it. He'd had enough of Dartmouth, he said, and, frankly, he'd had enough of our family.

'You can't do that. Not on your own,' Mum said.

'I won't be on my own. I'm moving in with my girlfriend,' Damo said.

'What girlfriend?' Mum said.

'The one I'm moving in with,' Damo said, and refused to tell us any more, save that the lack of bedrooms in the Above Town house (which he loved, by the way) needn't stand in our way.

Mum looked shocked, but Dad looked almost pleased, folding his arms and saying, 'Well, there you are, then,' as if what he meant was *end of argument*. It wasn't exactly the most tactful thing he could have done. Mum demanded to know how he could behave like that in the face of their firstborn moving in somewhere miles away with an unknown girl, and all because of arguments that, when it came down to it, were entirely his fault.

She didn't speak to him for days. Damo tried convincing her that, at his great age, he might have wanted his own place anyway. But Mum wasn't having it. The world was changing – and Dad was to blame.

I remember getting into a conversation with Judith Mason, of all people, on that subject. The changing world, I mean, not Mum and Dad. Judith might have had her faults, taking over people's gardens whether they wanted her to or not, but she was a damn good listener. She had this way of understanding what you hadn't even said and answering questions that you hadn't even asked her yet.

So when I said the world was changing and I didn't like it, she knew exactly what I meant.

'I feel so lost,' I said. 'Things are going on beyond my control. And it's all behind closed doors. Everything's a secret.'

Judith smiled sadly at that. As if she understood completely, she said that openness was a great thing but sometimes people had to have their secrets. Secrets made them feel safe.

'What do you mean?' I said, thinking of Frankie, certain that Judith was too – although when I look back, I'm not so sure.

'I mean that sometimes secrets are a person's way of coping in a changing world,' Judith said. 'They provide a way of staying in control.'

This was going way above my head. I said something about just wanting to get hold of the truth. Judith said truth was a tricky subject, meaning different things to different people, and you never knew where it might end up.

When she said that, a shiver ran through me. I thought of me pretending I wanted openness but running hard to get away from it, and Frankie wanting to tell me things but not knowing how. Perhaps the thing that kept us going was the performance we were putting on. Perhaps it wasn't that either of us was running away from anything, but that by doing things in a certain way, talking obliquely, sometimes even acting as if nothing was wrong, we'd found the means to cope.

I put this to Judith and she said maybe. It was an extraordinary conversation. I remember exactly where it took place, up the garden between rows of runner-bean canes and pea sticks. Suddenly I found the courage to ask all sorts of things about Frankie's condition that I hadn't dared to ask before and Judith explained as best she could. The cancer was spreading, she said, and there was nothing that could be done. Some days Frankie would feel bad and other days better, and there were drugs to help with the pain, and a vast range of other options too to improve the quality of her life.

'Cancer care has advanced in leaps and bounds,' Judith said. 'But nothing's going to effect a cure at this late stage.'

'Except for a miracle,' I said.

Judith pulled a face. 'The biggest miracle at this stage,' she said, 'would be for Frankie to slip away at peace with herself. What she really needs is to find a way of letting go. And you need to find that too. It's important to fight on your friend's behalf, and to think positive. But it's important to recognise the inevitable. Which brings us back to where we started. Change. Our world is changing, and we don't like it. But we have to learn to live with it, I'm afraid. There's nothing else we can do.'

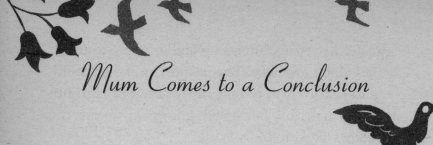

Mum Comes to a Conclusion

Not long after that conversation, Frankie went into hospital for a few days to sort out the level of calcium in her blood. Immediately the news went round Dartmouth that she'd gone in to die, and all sorts of people started coming up to me to ask about her.

I'd thought our friendship was still more or less secret, but apparently not. Suddenly, to my horror, I was a celebrity. People weren't just sorry for Frankie. Much to my astonishment, they were sorry for me. Even Bryony Rogers was. Suddenly (I shudder remembering it) she was all over me.

That weekend when Frankie was in hospital, Bryony dragged me off to Totnes to go round the shops. I didn't want to go, but Mum thought it would be good for me and even volunteered to drive us there. The two of us spent hours mooching up and down the little streets and rummaging through the market, trying things on and listening to music that I didn't even like. The purpose of it all, according to Bryony, was to take my mind off things. But that didn't stop her from going on about the Bradleys *all the time*.

She wanted to know everything – not just about Frankie but about her parents and, of course, her brothers. And then there was their house. Did they really have an avenue of palm trees, like some people said? And what did I mean when I said they had no swimming pool? Everybody in Dartmouth knew the Bradleys had a swimming pool. And what about their tennis court – had I played on it? Had I ridden any of their horses? And what about the view? Was it really as sensational as everybody said?

I trailed round Totnes, imagining a life beyond Frankie, where all I had for friends were people like Bryony Rogers. It was a grim prospect, and so was the prospect of my only value to society being as the friend of somebody who'd died.

We returned home on the bus, me in a state of total depression, only to find that between dropping us off in Totnes and my returning home, Mum had spent the afternoon locked in a row with Dad about the proposed house move. In the end, he'd gone storming off and Damo – who'd sat through most of it – said he didn't blame him. He couldn't wait to move to Plymouth, he said. In fact, he was counting the days.

Dad didn't come home for hours and an awful atmosphere hung over the house. Then, when he did come in, he was really funny with us all and wouldn't speak. I went and shut myself in my bedroom, where, not knowing who else to take it out on, I raged against God. I'd done my best, I said. I'd done everything I could. I'd prayed, tied ribbons to lamp posts, even tried to be open and face the truth head on. But where had any of it got me? And why did life have to be so difficult?

It's hard being angry with an ordinary person, like you or me. Someone you've got to face every day – that's hard enough. But being angry with God, who you can't see, or touch or even know for sure is there – the anger then is ten times worse. There's nobody to hit. No one to blame. No heart to break with cruel words. The only heart you break's your own.

I raged for days after that. Frankie came back home from hospital, her calcium levels sorted out, but there was no way I could go up and see her. She phoned asking for me, but I made excuses. I was always busy with other things and said I'd come tomorrow, and then tomorrow again.

According to Judith, Frankie was missing me. But

how was I meant to face her when I knew I couldn't keep up my cheery act? According to Judith, I had to bow to the inevitable. But it just wasn't possible. All I wanted to do was rage.

Frankie, in the meantime, was feeling much better. Going to the hospital had done her good and I was glad to hear it. One day her parents took her out on their boat. Another time they took her on a couple of short shopping trips. One afternoon they even took her riding in the woods.

Judith couldn't stop smiling when she told me about that. It was wonderful, she said, to see Frankie in the saddle, looking as if she was enjoying herself. It was obvious that Frankie wasn't just a job to Judith. Everybody said that Frankie couldn't have had a better nurse, and they were right.

Even Mum said it. She came home from seeing the Bradleys out somewhere and said that, in a funny sort of way, what she'd witnessed of Judith's care of Frankie reminded her of how she was in our garden.

'It's the attention to detail that one notices,' Mum said. 'Every little thing matters. Every little thing counts. Frankie's blossoming like a flower and you can quite see why. You know, I hate to say it but I was wrong about Judith Mason. I've been giving it a lot of thought. I've got this way of jumping to conclusions.

The Above Town house, for example. I was wrong about that and I'm wrong about Judith too. She's just a kindly person who's full of love.'

Juggling with Words

The following day after school, I went up to see Frankie and apologise for not going round for a while. I found her on a daybed in the garden, a pile of school books spread out around her, although she wasn't reading them. We sat out until the evening, when bats came swooping through the garden, then I took the last ferry home.

It was good to see Frankie again. The rage was gone and that was good as well, although a strange sadness hung over me that I couldn't shake off.

I went up almost every day after that. Sometimes Frankie was asleep and I didn't stay, but sometimes she was in high old spirits and we did all sorts of things together. She never seemed to have much energy, but we certainly made the most of what she'd got. We'd sit together watching boats coming in and out of the harbour. Sometimes we'd fantasise about being down in Castle Cove and, when we were sure no one was about, we'd talk to each other in our secret language.

Sometimes we even made up jokes in it and put them in the book. Frankie said that a joke that worked was as good as any poem. And she should know – that poem she'd recited down on the beach had proved to be the first of many.

I remember marvelling that, as certain of Frankie's skills seemed to die, new ones sprang up in their place. 'Whoever thought you'd end up a poet?' I said.

'I'm not sure that what I do is poetry. All I'm doing is juggling with words,' she said.

'What is poetry if not juggling with words?' I said. 'Don't knock yourself. You're the nearest Dartmouth's got to a Poet Laureate.'

Frankie laughed at that and changed the subject, saying, 'Let's play cards.' We played Shit-head, which I'd learnt from Damo and knew well enough to beat her hollow, and she taught me Rummy, but I won that too.

'Anybody else would let a poor sick girl win at least sometimes,' she complained.

'A poor sick girl? Who are you talking about?' I replied.

One afternoon, I arrived to find oxygen installed by Frankie's bed, and other bits of machinery, which nobody explained. Frankie didn't mention them, so I didn't either. I'd go up there sometimes and she'd have an oxygen mask on, but we'd watch telly as if nothing was out of the ordinary. Sometimes she was even attached to a drip, which we'd wheel round wherever we went, but never talk about.

These things began to feel almost like ordinary life. I knew they weren't, of course, but it's amazing what you can get used to.

World War Three

There's one day in particular that stands out in my mind. It began ordinarily enough, with me going up to Bradley Castle to watch telly with Frankie and her falling asleep. Mr Bradley volunteered to drive me down to the ferry, which was something he normally never did.

I said that I could walk, but Mr Bradley insisted and, on the way down, he suddenly announced how much he appreciated my friendship with his daughter. I was embarrassed, and I think he must have been too, because his voice went all hoarse and awkward, and I even wondered for a moment if he might be trying not to cry.

'There's nothing to thank me for,' I said. 'Really, you don't have to.'

Mr Bradley smiled at that. I was selling myself short, he said. I knew what he was talking about, and knew what I had done, and it had meant the world to Frankie, and the rest of them. 'We all think you're a treasure,' he said. 'Mrs Bradley, George, Diggory – we all feel the same, and we want you to know.'

When I got home, the first thing I did was tell Mum. She was busy in the kitchen, juggling supper, housework and the week's ironing. She said, 'Charis, that's wonderful . . .' but I don't think she really took in what I was saying because, the next thing I knew, she was thrusting an empty linen basket at me and asking me to bring in the dry things off the washing line.

'Oh, and look for your dad while you're about it,' she said. 'He's up there somewhere and it's time to eat.'

I went up the garden feeling slightly deflated. The washing line was at the top, behind the laurel hedge. I made my way towards it, taking the short cut round the side of the pigpen. And that's where I found Dad.

Snogging Judith Mason.

Actually, Dad was doing more than snogging. Groping's probably a better word – and Judith Mason was groping him back. Pressed up against the pigpen, they were both at each other. Dad's hands were up Judith's T-shirt and hers were in his hair, tugging at chunks of it while she sucked at his face.

I dropped the linen basket – not that anybody noticed. 'Oh, God, no . . .' I thought, and my first reaction was shame, as if *I* was the one who'd been caught out. But my second reaction was Mum. *What would happen if she saw?*

I turned my head instinctively, checking that she was still safely in the kitchen – and that was when Damo appeared. Where he'd come from, I don't know. But suddenly he was right behind me and he saw Dad and Judith too, and that's when World War Three broke out.

Damo Big-Mouth – he couldn't help himself. He let out the biggest yell, and Mum came tearing out of the house, thinking there'd been an accident. She came running up towards us and Dad and Judith Mason leapt apart as if they'd had an electric shock.

But they were too late. Already Mum was halfway up the garden and she'd seen enough.

As a moment of pure drama, it was unsurpassable. Looking back, I can almost see it in that light. But at the time it was a bloodbath, nothing more, nothing less. Like a missile hitting its target, Mum exploded. There was nothing anyone could do to stop her.

We all tried, of course. Damo grabbed Mum, doing his best to hold her back. And Dad went rushing down to her, trying to explain. But Mum hurled herself at him and started hitting and shouting. She drowned him out, and drowned out Judith too, who was struggling to explain as well.

Not that anything she said could have made any difference. Of course it was what it looked like! And who cared that she was sorry? And so what that she hadn't meant it to happen, not like that? So what that neither of them had?

'*You pig!*' Mum screamed at Dad. 'You *bitch!*' she screamed at Judith. Her face was bright red. Rage was spitting out of her in white flecks.

Between them, Dad and Damo got her into the kitchen and slammed the door. Dad was crying, and I was too. Judith took one look at me and fled. Through the kitchen door I could hear Damo calling Judith a witch and Mum calling Dad a false betrayer. I couldn't face them. I didn't want to know what would happen next. I couldn't bear Mum's expression of total betrayal or Dad's weaselly guilt.

So I sneaked round to Grandma's side of the house and stayed there for the rest of the day. I went without supper and watched telly in Grandma's chair, as if trying to glean comfort from it, and even slept in her bed. For much of the night, I could hear Mum and Dad going on at each other through the wall. Every time I woke up they were still at it.

Next morning, however, when I went round to

get my school bag and change my clothes, an uneasy silence hung about the place. I found Mum and Dad sitting at the kitchen table not saying anything, while Damo was leaning in the doorway, as if he couldn't make up his mind whether to go or stay.

I went and stood with him, and he put his arm around my shoulder. Good old Damo! Dad said we had to talk. I said I didn't see why. Dad said he loved us. I said he'd got a funny way of showing it.

'I'm sorry,' Dad said, looking terrible. 'Believe me, I am. But sometimes things go wrong. It's hard to explain. Things feel different. A parent dies. Not that I'm making excuses, but lines get crossed. Arguments end up meaning more than they should. These things happen, I'm afraid. People find themselves doing things they shouldn't. But that doesn't mean they can't be put right.'

I didn't want things put right. My dad was a false betrayer, like Mum had said. I told myself I wanted him to go away and never come back.

'Are you and Mum breaking up?' I said, hoping that the answer would be yes.

'Of course we're not,' said Dad.

I looked at Mum. She shook her head, but I didn't know what that meant. Dad got up and took a step towards me. Instinctively, I put Damo between us. Immediately Dad sat down again. I glared at him, thinking that I'd never be able to look at him again without seeing Judith Mason hanging off him. I hated him – but that was nothing compared to what I felt for her. Dad might be a false betrayer. *But she was worse.*

'I could just *kill* somebody,' I said.

Nobody needed to ask who I meant. Dad flushed. This was all his fault, he said, not poor Judith's. She was going through a terrible time just now, what with Frankie Bradley slipping away and that brother of hers, whose marriage had broken up and he had no one else to live with.

'What brother?' Mum said.

'Your choir leader friend,' Dad said. 'John Bepp.'

'But he's her toy boy,' Mum said. 'That's what everybody says.'

'Well, everybody's got it wrong,' said Dad. 'He's Judith's brother, believe me.'

I glanced at Mum. Could Dad be right? She said nothing, just gave a small shrug indicating that it made no difference either way. As if he thought he'd been given permission or something, Dad carried on about Judith – how she was a person just like us, trying to make sense of a difficult world, who happened to have been there for him when he was feeling low. Not that there was anything serious between them, he hastened to assure us. Just that one crazy moment. Just a kiss that had got out of hand.

But I wasn't having it – and neither was Mum.

'*Out of hand*?' she cried. 'Is that what you call it?'

And suddenly they were at it again, neither listening to the other. Mum started crying in great noisy gulps, like a drowning woman gasping for air. I went and put my arms round her, but I don't think she even noticed me.

In the end, I crept away. I should have gone to school, but I went up to Frankie's house instead. I needed my friend. Crossing on the ferry, I didn't even notice what a fabulous morning it was, warm and golden, a perfect day for bunking off school. My head was reeling and I felt sick. What if Mum and Dad did break up? Whatever I'd thought earlier, I didn't really want that to happen.

When I arrived at Bradley Castle, I found the gates open, allowing me to walk in unannounced. Normally the Bradleys are amazingly particular about matters of security, but this little lapse of theirs couldn't have happened on a better day. I went round the side of the house, hoping to get into the Snug without meeting anyone on the way. As I crossed the top terrace however, suddenly there was Frankie right in front of me, her bed wheeled out so that she could enjoy the sun.

I fetched a chair and went and sat beside her. Good old Frankie! She was always there for me, even though – like now – she might appear asleep. I took her hand. It felt cold and her breathing was laboured, like a rower's on a winter river. Settling down beside her, I started talking as if I knew she was awake really and could hear me. What had happened to that stable girl that her father had had an affair with? Had he ever seen her again, or had it all petered out? And what about her parents' divorce? Had she heard any more about that? And did they still argue, or had that all stopped?

When Frankie didn't answer, I explained what had happened in my own family. I didn't tell her that the evil witch in question was Judith Mason, her own nurse, but I told her everything else and was just about finishing when Mrs Bradley came out onto the terrace to check on her daughter.

As soon as I heard her coming, I darted under the bed. It was an odd thing to do, I'll grant you that, but I was totally incapable of facing anybody or explaining why I'd bunked off school. And Frankie understood. I was sure of that. She might appear asleep, but she even thought the whole thing was funny. I could have sworn she did, because I was certain I heard her stifle a giggle.

For ages after that, I was stuck under the bed. Mrs

Bradley started fussing over Frankie and wouldn't leave her alone. Then one of the nurses – who could have been Judith Mason, but could equally have been one of Frankie's other round-the-clock carers – came out too, and they had a hushed conversation I couldn't catch. Then Mrs Bradley sat in my chair and started whispering to Frankie – again things I couldn't catch.

She did it for so long that eventually I fell asleep. It was hot under the bed, and the sound of her voice lulled me. But then the last twenty-four hours had done for me anyway. I wasn't so much tired as completely wiped out.

I awoke later to find that the sun had moved, the garden was full of shadows that hadn't been there before and the day felt different. No longer was it just Mrs Bradley at Frankie's bedside. All of them were there – Diggers, George, Mr Bradley, even Dr Herbert. When he walked back to the house, I watched him go. It was the first time I'd seen him in the flesh. And Frankie was right. He *was* more handsome than Orlando Bloom.

Not that I would ever be able to tell her.

Because Frankie was dead.

At first I didn't realise. People were coming and going, and I could hear some of them crying and others saying that they hadn't expected this, not yet.

And I thought that they were joking. I know this sounds incredible, but I remembered Frankie's giggle and thought that any minute now her face would appear under the bed and she'd cry out, 'Gotcha,' or something like that.

But then Diggers spoke in a sad, grave voice that didn't have a hint of jokiness in it. 'Look at the trees,' he said. 'Look at the river, and the sea and the sky. *What a way to go.*'

His voice was awestruck. And then I knew this was for real. What a way to go indeed! I remained under the bed until they'd all returned inside. If they'd wheeled Frankie back in I'd have been discovered, but they left her where she was, as if they couldn't bring themselves to deprive her skin of the last warmth of the sun.

And this gave me the chance to make my escape. I crept out from under the bed, almost believing that I could still hear Frankie giggling and yet knowing that it wasn't possible.

Frankie would have loved all this, I thought, standing over the bed. If she'd planned it herself, it couldn't have worked out better. She might have gone, but her sense of humour definitely lived on. This was one for the joke book, no doubt about that.

'Have you heard the one about the girl under the

bed, who came to tell her friend her secrets?' I whispered before I left. 'Well, the last laugh was on her, because the friend was dead.'

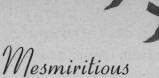

Mesmiritious

Frankie didn't get *mesmiritious* spelt out in flowers, like she wanted. Nobody took this seriously, funnily enough. But she got the cremation she had asked for, with her ashes sprinkled afterwards in Castle Cove. And all the right bequests went to all the right people. I made sure of that.

To this day, nobody knows about me being under Frankie's bed. I somehow managed to escape without being seen and, when Mrs Bradley phoned later to say that Frankie had gone, I pretended I didn't know.

In fact, writing this down in the latest of my Pillar's notebooks is the first time I've admitted what really took place that day. Maybe no one will ever read it, but at least I've owned up.

There's one last thing I want to write and then I'm done. I could have put it in before, but it fits in better here. Apart from anything else, this is how I want to remember Frankie, not as a pile of ashes, even if sprinkled in Castle Cove.

It's something that the two of us did after she came out of hospital, when her calcium levels had been sorted out and we were having that golden period when I went up all the time. Remember Mr Bradley saying that the family appreciated what I'd done for Frankie? Well this, in particular, was what he had in mind.

Somewhere round that time, Frankie's parents found out about the sky-diving day. Maybe it came up about Diggers missing school, I can't quite remember, but I do remember reckoning I had some explaining to do. Frankie's parents said something about remembering Frankie wanting to be a pilot when she was younger, and out it all came about her secret flying dream, and how she felt about freedom, flight and laughter, and how I'd tried to fly for her, linking my fear of flying with her fear of death.

And Frankie's parents got it. They put the pieces all together and understood. Not only that, but they recognised that even at this advanced stage in Frankie's illness something could be done. I said that, in my opinion, Frankie still needed to fly and they agreed with me. Then I told them about the balloons I'd seen that day drifting over the Severn estuary and, being the Bradleys, they went out and bought one of their own.

It wasn't good enough to hire one; they had to own it. They also had to hire the services of a world-class balloon pilot and the back-up services of his company for an extraordinary journey across the sky.

The whole thing had to be a surprise, though. Frankie wasn't to know what was being planned. Her parents booked Sunday tea in a country house hotel, billing it as a family celebration for George and Diggers because their exams were over. But even they didn't know what was going to happen after the last cucumber sandwich had been put away.

The hotel had a big lawn at the front, which was where we sat, and an even bigger one at the back, where the pilot and his helpers prepared the launch site. After we'd finished eating, we strolled round to find a recovery truck sitting on the grass, its back open and a massive wicker basket being lifted out.

Frankie's parents headed straight towards it.

'What's going on?' Frankie said.

'I don't know,' I said.

Diggers laughed at that. I shrugged as if to say, *Nothing to do with me*, but he gave me a look as if he knew that I was lying. By now the basket had been unloaded and the pilot was making his way across the lawn to introduce himself. He had the greyest eyes I'd ever seen. Like steel they were, hard and still and shining. He introduced his team, which included a straggly-haired woman who was in charge of the recovery truck and another, younger, woman whose name was Bonnie and would be flying with us.

'I don't understand,' Frankie said. 'What do you mean, *flying with us?*'

The pilot smiled. So did Mr and Mrs Bradley. So did Diggers, who laughed again, and George, who whooped with delight.

'Welcome to your maiden flight,' the pilot said.

Frankie shrieked. But before she could fly anywhere, first the Bradleys' new balloon had to be launched. This involved connecting the wicker basket to a wrinkled heap of blue cloth by means of a network of steel cables, hauling over two massive fans and setting up an electricity generator.

The pilot was in charge of the inflation, but he had a younger man there to help him, who was as quick and light as air. Together they spread the blue cloth out on the ground and instructed us to move round it carefully, shaking it out so that every corner could be filled. Then Frankie and Mrs Bradley were positioned on one side of the balloon's mouth and Mr Bradley on the other, and they were shown how to hold up its rim to let in air.

Finally the pilot switched on the fans – and immediately the balloon started growing. Its midnight blue cloth billowed out across the hotel lawn like a sea full of waves. In no time at all, it had opened out and looked big enough inside to host a wedding party. Then the pilot took a roaring propane burner and directed a jet of flame, as hot and angry as dragon's breath, into the balloon's mouth.

The result was dramatic. As soon as the air inside started heating up, the balloon began to rise. Its reaction to heat was instantaneous. Until now it had simply bobbed about on the ground, its basket lying motionless on its side. Now, however, as the balloon lifted, the basket started tilting into an upright position. Finally both balloon and basket were ready.

Frankie was the first person to be lifted in, with the grey-eyed pilot and her father dancing in attendance. The rest of the Bradleys, however, had to climb in for themselves.

'Come on,' called the pilot, once Frankie was in and comfortable. 'Quickly – we've got no time to waste.'

The Bradleys stepped forward, but I stepped back. This was Frankie's treat, not mine. Never once, in any of our secret planning sessions, had I said I'd fly as well.

But Frankie wasn't flying without me – and nor was anybody else. 'Where do you think you're going?' everybody called as I headed for the recovery truck.

The next thing I knew, I was being hauled into the basket and wedged onto a bench seat between Frankie and Diggory.

'You don't understand . . .' I kept on saying. But all they did was laugh at me and say I'd be all right and that they'd hold my hand.

There was no way I could get out of it. The younger woman, Bonnie, explained about the launch position that we had to take, sitting side by side until the balloon was safely in the air. As far as I was concerned, though, I'd have stayed like that forever, keeping my head down and my eyes closed. But Frankie wouldn't let me.

It all happened so quickly. We'd hardly got off the ground before she was on her feet. The pilot directed the burner into the balloon's mouth for another blast of heat and Frankie was up to watch the balloon straining on its tether, the basket swaying from side to side.

Everybody gasped.

'Sit down, please,' the pilot called to Frankie, but she simply couldn't do it.

Another blast of heat and the basket lifted clean

off the ground. Frankie hauled me up as well, to see what was happening. Then Bonnie unclipped the cable that kept us tethered to the recovery truck and that was it. We were airborne. We were flying. *Flying*.

The launch field fell beneath us like a stone down a well. And so did my fear of flying, extraordinarily enough. I can't believe the way it went, just like that. But there was so much to look at, I had no time to be afraid.

I'd always known the world was big, but never this big. The hotel lawn disappeared beneath us, caught up in a wider world that seemed to have no end. Soon I couldn't see it any more, or pick out the hotel. Somewhere down there we'd enjoyed Sunday tea, but now that place was gone.

The view from the basket was awesome. I tried to find the road we'd driven in on, but it was impossible to locate. Everything was different up here in the air. Nothing looked familiar anymore. Our pilot explained that this was partly due to the speed we were travelling at, carried away from everything we might recognise by a brisk breeze.

But this only confused me. I couldn't feel any speed. Everything up in the air seemed calm and still. In fact, we hardly seemed to be moving.

'What breeze?' I said. Looking round, I couldn't

even see a hair stirring on anybody's head.

Our pilot smiled, as if he understood why I might be confused. 'Just because you can't *see* the breeze, it doesn't mean to say there isn't one,' he said. 'It's simply that, travelling as we are, we've become a part of it. Think about it for a minute. If we were stationary, we'd feel the full force of the wind buffeting us. But because we're moving with it, there's nothing to feel. In the heart of the wind, we're perfectly still.'

I'll always remember those words. Sometimes things get said that really strike you and this was one of those occasions. Frankie's illness was like a wind, I thought. We were all being swept along by it and yet we'd found this place of stillness at its heart.

I remember feeling wonderfully at peace after that. Wonderfully safe, in a way that makes no sense when you think about what we were doing. I looked down and the world beneath the basket was spread out like an open book waiting to be read. I'd prayed for openness and now I'd got it in bucket loads. Everything was plain to see. There were no secrets in the world below me. I could see everything for what it was. And I mean *everything*.

Until that flight, I never knew that the county I grew up in had so many hills, valleys, rivers, lakes, houses, gardens, villages and towns. I never knew it had so many trees either, or that they came in so many different shades of green. A pair of riders beneath us moved into the balloon's shadow and looked up. Some children in a garden waved and we waved back. Sheep in a field ran back and forth, startled by our roaring burner. A farm dog went crazy, jumping and barking as if trying to convince the fire-belching dragon in the sky that it wasn't afraid.

Then our pilot, master showman that he was, decided to demonstrate something new. At first we didn't realise what was happening, only that he was working the burners and things beneath us were becoming harder to pick out.

Clouds started appearing around us and to begin with we tried to see through them. Soon, however, it became impossible. In just a few short minutes we found ourselves surrounded by cloud formations and strange misty vapours. The sun still shone through them, but everything was cast in a different light.

It was a wonderful light too. There were kingdoms in that light – castles in the clouds, mountains of melting whiteness on every side of us and mountains of gold, blurring the distinction between earth and sky. Once I'd thought of Castle Cove as a kingdom, but it was nothing compared to this.

I looked at Frankie and she looked back. Then

our steel-eyed pilot took us up again until the clouds fell beneath us. Here the sky above gave a whole new meaning to the word *blue*. It was so fresh, that sky. So delicate and perfect. So clear that anything I'd seen before seemed like a muddy pond.

'Mesmiritious,' murmured Frankie.

'As good as it gets,' I agreed. 'Yes.'

Later in our flight, old Steel-Eyes told us that we'd been over a mile above the ground. The point he was trying to make was that a mile's a long way. But it was so different up there that it could have been a million miles, as far as I was concerned. It could have been the other side of space.

For the rest of the flight, we travelled at far lower heights. The balloon came down through the clouds and the earth beneath us became clear again, glistening with water caught in the evening sun. Long shadows fell across fields and valleys as our flight drew towards its end.

We were getting lower all the time, looking for a place to land. Bonnie was on the radio, liaising with the recovery truck. Mr Bradley was pointing out possible landing points as if, with an hour's balloon flight under his belt, he was suddenly an expert. Mrs Bradley was going on about not wanting the flight to end, and so were George and Diggers.

But Frankie said nothing. She hadn't spoken since

she'd said the word mesmiritious. But then, what else was there to say?

By now we were close enough to almost reach down and touch the trees as we drifted over them, even, incredibly, glimpsing birds in their nests. Above us, I could see the first star of evening shining serenely and, for a brief moment, I felt as if the two of us, that star and I, were fellow travellers on the same ocean, seeing the world through the same eyes.

Then suddenly the field ahead of us was the right one. There were no pylons cutting it in half. It wasn't full of stubble that would tear the balloon to shreds. Mr Bradley was crying, 'Go, go, go . . .' and Bonnie was calling for us to take up our landing positions.

We came down as softly as a feather – and the very first thing I wanted to do was go back up! The sky was above me again and the earth lay at my feet, cool and solid. Everything was as it should be and as it always had been – and yet nothing felt the same.

And it never has done, if I'm honest with myself.

Going up there changed me. It changed the way I look at life and the way I think. Once I let go and dared to fly. And I did it for myself, not anybody else. I didn't fly for Frankie. She flew for herself. And I lost my fear and, out there on the far horizon of everything she'd known, she lost hers. We made a few discoveries about ourselves. Everything was different from what we'd thought. We'd peeled back the edges of our world and found out there was more.

Deflating the balloon was quickly done, but it was dark by the time we'd finished. A pair of headlights came across the field towards us, accompanied by the droning sound of the recovery truck labouring over difficult ground. When it reached us, it backed right up to the basket, then the driver leapt out and started getting things packed up and loaded.

We rushed to help, everybody piling in. In no time at all, everything was safely stored in the back of the truck. Then someone produced a bottle of champagne and everybody toasted everybody else's good health, including Frankie's, who was so exhausted by this stage that she'd clambered into the front seat, and was already half-asleep, a smile on her face.